The Forgotten Queen

S.L. Simmons

Book cover: S.L. Simmons via Canva
Interior: S.L. Simmons via Canva

first edition, July 2025

www.slsimmonswordsmith.com

CONTENTS

This Book Contains

For Content & Trigger Warnings
and
Genre/Trope Listing
visit

www.slsimmonswordsmith.com

*Straighten your crown, strike those matches,
and burn it the fuck down.*

Special Edition

Numbered Limited Edition Hardbacks
with artist rendered cover available.
Each has sprayed edges and
decorative chapter artwork.

Contact S.L. Simmons for availability.

To The Reader

Hello Dearest Reader,

In the worlds that spin in my head, the characters tell the tales. I am just the medium they use to bring their lives to the light. Sometimes an image inspires, sometimes a movie or show, but mostly music. The escape scene was inspired by the song *This Is How Villains Are Made* by Madalen Duke. For some time I only had that scene in my head, not sure where to use it in the worlds that swirl in the ether that is my brain. A pastiche of Wonderland slowly came to life and here we are.

The Forgotten Queen is a spin off from the classic tales by Lewis Carroll. You will recognize many characters and places. However, I did say it was a spin off. The time frame is forward from Alice's adventures. Many are descendants of Mister Carroll's creations.

The bandersnatch are big cat shifters. Unlike many shifter stories, they don't have knots. They do have their own special adaptation though. They form prides, not packs, but are still ruled by an alpha based hierarchy. Bandersnatch can be warriors or priests. Warriors protect the Temple of the Underland. Priests are mentors to young banders (cubs) and see to prayers, deals, and payments. Should a bandersnatch's beast be repressed, a cheshire forms. Underlanders want to live in peace with their land like the original peoples.

The Horunvendush is the kingdoms collectively and at one time was the main trade center before the division. The Providence of the Pale and The Crimson Dynasty have divided Underland between the two dating back to Carroll's story of red versus white. They rule with their armies of Deck and Board. The people who live under them are called Dush. Dush are descendants of Underland that are not bandersnatch mixed with human.

Humans still come and go, some stay, some just leave something behind. Humans are from Overland. All call them Wanderers.

You're going to meet Devana (Deh-vah-nuh). This is her story. Or is it?

S.L. Simmons

p.s.
Remember to go to my website for the trigger and trope lists. Mental health matters, even when the tale is one of madness.

What is a state where reason is lost,
logic is shattered,
and thoughts dance wildly,
leaving behind only chaos and confusion?

Powers That Be

"Push!"

"I am, you fucking bitch!"

"If you don't get that child out of you, neither of you will make it through the night."

"If you had rid me of it any of the other times I came to you, I wouldn't be here doing this. Do something to get this godsdamned thing out of me."

Katya stood at the foot of the platform the woman writhed on as she struggled to push her child into the world. Handing a thick rope that was tied to either of the legs at the foot where she stood, she instructed the woman to pull on it while pressing her heels into the footing board to assist in bearing down. Groans and grunts turned to screams as the babe finally crowned. With a last push, a pale bundle slid into the world.

Silence greeted the pair. Peeling a cowl off the face of the still infant, Katya laid it on the bed and rubbed it vigorously to get it to cry.

"Leave it, Crone."

"I need to stimulate so breath will come."

"I said leave it. Attend me. I need to return immediately. That is not what I was promised. I was promised a son. As you can see, that is not a male child. A female cannot inherit the throne. I needed an heir to rule."

With an eye on the still babe, Katya did as she was instructed. A queen's decree was not to be ignored. It could cost one their head. When the small chest took a shudder followed by a whimper, a breath of relief left her. Placing a towel on the tiny creature in the hopes it would keep her warm until she could tend it, Katya returned to doing as she was ordered.

The rattle of the carriage hadn't even faded from the clearing where her home sat before she was rushing back inside. Grabbing the child and a pile of clean rags, Katya crashed to her knees before her hearth. Laying the child on the rug, she shoved two chunks of wood into the dying flames, rocking them back and forth into the coals to get them to catch. Pulling the pot she kept on the edge to keep hot water always on hand closer, Katya set to work.

***

Sliding from the back of her horse was not an easy feat when there was a child strapped to her chest, but Katya did so without a stumble or squashing the babe. With a nod to the lad that had grabbed the reins when she rode into the yard, Katya made her way through the small village that cared for Temple. The cobbles were icy from the last storm, making the short walk longer with the care to where she had to place her footing.

Never one to want children, having one in her care that was not in need of her healing skills had Katya's nerves set on high. She herself was not the offspring of the last Crone. All she could remember of how she came to be in the care of Crone was standing before a wooden door, waiting for it to open.

4

A thin, wizened woman had wretched the panel open, surprise on her face at finding Katya there, before looking about. None other than the waif of a girl was on that strip of roofed dirt in the front of the house. Eyes still shrewd for her advanced years, Crone had given a sniff, rearing back at whatever she had smelled. With a curtsy, she welcomed Katya in and taught her the craft. But that was far longer ago than many could remember.

She was to be a spinster like those before her that showed an affinity for caring and healing those that came calling. Now she was not a virgin. No, she had sampled many a male, man and woman. The call of those nights when she sought out more than what she could relieve herself were few, but they kept her memories ripe with images to keep her going until the next time. A few herbs and not a babe grew in her own body. It had been drummed into her by her predecessor that a family of her own to care for would take from the time she had to give those more needing of her talents.

Here Katya found herself now strapped with a child that she knew not how to care for nor, in truth, wanted. Far beyond the years when her womb had called for just this thing. Entering the foyer, she stopped before a grouping of boys that were playing on the floor. Orphans, payment for services, indentured, all were raised to one day be the next generation of warriors for their gods. Pulling the knot on her shoulder, she handed the babe to the tallest of the bunch that came to stand at her approach. "Mind her well."

Nose wrinkling, the boy looked down into the sleeping face in the crook of his arm. "She? Crone, no female is permitted to be housed in Temple. They cannot withstand the ways of males."

With a snort at the cub referring to himself as if a full grown male, Katya made her way to the altar and the doors to either side of it.

The door closing behind her echoed in the cavernous room in front of her. Nothing from the outside gave away the intent that was housed here. Deep magic pulled at her feet once she shed her shoes and stepped onto the soft ground in front of her. Sucking a breath so large it nearly made her cough, Katya stood tall, shedding her cloak and glamour.

What the outside world saw as a plain older woman became a mature woman of natural beauty. Shaking the strands of her hair loose from her braid, the silver faded to match the dark mink brown of her eyebrows. Clouded eyes became a clear blue like the sky at the height of summer. Wrinkles, spots, and lines dissolved into a youthful glow. The fabric of her clothing rustled as it hit the moss she tread on. Hidden under the layers was the voluptuous body of a nymph.

"Absolem." Voice a clear tone now instead of a scratch that others heard, Katya called out into the space.

Stepping from her clothing pile, she tread forward. The ground was covered in soft moss with stone islands scattered around. Large trees made the pillars that held the roof, birds and small creatures darting among the branches. If one did not know better, they would think they were outside with all the life that breathed power into the air around her.

Rustles of cloth came from her left. "My love, what brings you to me on this harsh winter day?"

With a smile for the male approaching, Katya took him in. He had not changed in all the years she had known him. He was far older than his looks told. He was old when she was but a girl. Now that she herself was advanced in years, he had to be well into being ancient. His body was fit, skin unmarred from time and battles. A healthy glow in spite of the time he spent here in the dappled light of the inner sanctum. The only thing that told of his age was the color of his hair. A shocking white that fell down to his waist in a sheet she was envious of with hers always a riot of curls.

Absolem removed the long vest from his own shoulders and placed it on Katya's. Falling to her calves where it dusted his thighs only enhanced the difference in their beings. The sleeves must have been a foot past her fingertips, only hitting him at his wrists. Looking up into the face of the only male she could say held her heart, Katya smiled. "I am on a mission to rake one of your priests over the coals."

Head tossed back, Absolem's booming laugh echoed around the chamber. Eyes twinkling with mirth, he wrapped his arms around Katya, pulling her into his chest, "I do not envy the male that has drawn your anger. What has one of my wayward children done this time?"

Mind quick to jump to the call of her body for him at his touch, she heaved a sigh, pushing aside that thump in her clit that begged for Aboslem's attention in favor of the business that had sent her from her home. Stepping from his arms, Katya turned towards the doors as if to walk back out in search of the male that was responsible. "I helped birth a babe last evening. The mother left it in my care. Ranting on how the deals with priests were not worth the air they were spoken with. Claiming she was promised a son but had birthed the opposite."

Absolem cocked his head and began walking next to Katya. "A deal broken? Not likely. They are given what they ask for. Who was the woman?"

"Ekaterina, Queen of the Pale."

The room fell silent. Not a creature made so much as a ruffle of feather or fur. The gentle breeze and notes that floated on it were hushed. The dapples of light faded so only the shadows inhabited.

Katya turned and looked to where Absolem stood as still as his sentinels. "What is it? Do you know of the arrangement?"

With a swift movement that had the linen pants he wore billowing behind him at the speed, Absolem turned from the main doors and strode into the gloom. Katya followed at a near run. Doors opened when they neared though no one manned them only to close with echoes into the chamber in front of them. The air grew colder, the feeling of descending unnerved Katya.

She had heard tales, told at the knee of her own Crone. Stories of what lay beneath the hallowed building. Whispers that scared even the strongest of males. A whimper escaped, causing Absolem to turn to her. "I need to see the Time Keeper. He will know what is to be done. You can remain in the sanctuary if this is too fearful for you. But I think that you will find what he says most useful and I wish for you to accompany me. I must warn you that you must never speak of where we are about to go."

Katya looked back the way they had come. High above them, she could just make out the light. How had they come so far, so fast? In front of Absolem was the deepest darkness she had ever gazed into. Wrapping her arms around herself, drawing the front of the vest closed over her naked body, Katya could not help the shiver that overtook her.

Absolem's hand stroked down her hair, the other tilted her chin up to look at him. "I will never take you into danger. Never. You have my word and my life in that promise."

At her nod of acceptance, Absolem pressed his lips to hers, deepening the kiss with a growl, he pulled away. "I should have ignored the message given and taken you before you even spoke the reason for today's visit. I long to feel your cunt wrapped around me, squeezing in your pleasure as I fill you. I love watching my cum leak out of you when I'm finished ravishing your body."

Swaying into his chest, Katya groaned at the picture he painted. "If wishes were horses..."

Wrapping her hand in his, Absolem pulled Katya into the dark below.

Bindings In Blood

"What is it?"

Leonid rolled his eyes at the boy next to him, "a baby."

With a shove to the shoulder of his twin on his other side for slapping him in the back of the head for whatever they deemed he said dumb now, Josef glared at the leader of their pride. "I know it is a baby and a girl. Heard Crone call it so. I was asking what is that...pull? Right here."

Leonid looked to where Josef was rubbing the center of his chest. Daniil was copying his twin, knuckling at the bone. Anatoli remained where they had left him, sitting against the wall, arms wrapped around his skinny legs, large eyes not leaving the bundle of cloth. "Toli? What is it?"

A quick flick of his eyes from the child to Leonid's and back. "She is different. Different like I am." Two more pairs of eyes landed on him as Josef and Daniil stopped moving long enough to listen. "Mine, ours. My...cat says so."

Leonid looked down to the sleeping infant in his arms. He was larger than the other two being older than them by some years, but Anatoli was older than him, just slighter due to his parentage. It wasn't just his age that made him wiser. He saw things. Knew things. Father said it was due to him being what he was.

11

A cheshire was different from what he and the others were. Rare. Powerful in ways a bandersnatch wasn't. That didn't stop others from picking at him. Where a bandersnatch was built for war, bulking out when maturity began like it had with Leonid and would for Josef and Daniil in a few years, Anatoli was slim, sleek, lean. And his animal. It wasn't like his pride mates. Never showing itself in full form or talking to him like a bandersnatch did. It was like its host; quiet, watchful. So when it spoke, they listened.

"Ours." Moving so he could kneel in front of his friend, Leonid motioned for the twins to join them. Moving the blankets from her face, he held her closer to the seated boy. "Do you want to see her?"

Anatoli moved to mimic Leonid, kneeling so they boxed her in. Pulling the blankets from her so he could see her better, they watched as her skin seemed to ripple when his hand brushed her arm, the veins going black before it dissipated like smoke. "See, different. He wants me to bite her. Show she is ours so no one hurts her. Protect her."

Leonid looked around the outer room they had been told to wait in. They were there for yet another punishment for fighting. None were paying attention, a group of older priests were around the pride that had started it, even though they got the worst end of it. Beaten badly even if they were older yet than Toli. The only mark on any of them was a scratch on Daniil when the oldest of the group had partially shifted a hand and clawed his face.

"Keep an eye out, Toli." Trusting his friends, Leonid pricked his finger on a canine before slipping it into the mouth of the babe. She wrinkled her little nose at him and tried to turn away before latching on and giving a suck. Popping his finger free, he nodded to Anatoli to do the same. Josef was ready with a bead of blood when it was his turn, Daniil following his brother. As Daniil finished, a shout came from across the room.

Glancing over his shoulder, Leonid looked into the angry eyes of one of the priests as he and his pride bore down on them. They were the mentors of the group they had fought. "What are you boys doing?"

There was no way he could smell the blood as the other pride was bleeding from several wounds. Something else must have set off his senses. Anatoli steadied Leonid as he stood so as not to drop the baby, other hands quickly tucking the blankets around her. "Nothing, sir. We were charged with the care of this babe by the crone. Don't know what to do with her."

The hall was silent.

"Her? She brought a girl child in here? Did she say how she came to have it?"

All attention in the hall was now on them. Leonid looked down to make sure they wouldn't be able to tell that they had sworn her into their pride the best they could without a bite. "No, sir. Only told me to care for her."

Moving to where the line of males motioned them into the center of the room, Leonid stood proud, holding the bundle so the light from the central opening spilled on her. Several snarls drew his attention from the tiny being in his arms. Lip curled, the priest that had called him forward, stepped back. "She doesn't smell right. Probably from being in that hag's care. Take her outside and wait there for you to be called back in."

Anatoli touched his elbow, looking to where he stood to the right like the beta he would become to him should, he saw a slight shake of his head. "Sir, it is cold. The babe is barely wrapped. The Crone brought her wrapped in her cloak to keep her warm."

The male in the speaker's own beta position leaned in and whispered in his ear. "Very well, return to where you were. Keep her quiet."

Josef leaned back against the wall, eyes watching the males as they met with another pride. His gift of reading lips at play. "They are questioning why she is here. They don't like the fact Crone comes and goes as she pleases. Angry that they are locked out of the inner sanctum when she is."

Leonid kept his back to the room, trusting his own to warn him should something come his way. He didn't want eyes on the baby and standing like he was, even making himself vulnerable, kept them off her. "Father knows what he is doing and if that means keeping his children from his inner fortress, then so be it. They know better than to question him. He knows what is in our hearts and minds before we do. Stupid males only win stupid prizes."

Daniil's hopeful eyes return to Anatoli, slouching back against the wall in front of Leonid, "does he say anything else Toli?"

All the boys were curious if Anatoli's cat would say more.

Anatoli's eyes go unfocused as he concentrates. Cocking his head like he is listening, he blinks up at Leonid, "he is purring."

Leonid steps closer, turning his head and focusing on removing the background sounds like he has been taught. Sure enough, Anatoli's cat is purring. His own joins in. He has never purred before. Growled, snarled, roared, chuffed, hissed, but never a purr. Looking at Josef and Daniil, who shake their heads, maybe they are too young, he locks eyes with Anatoli. His cat called her mine and his is saying the same. "They like her. I don't know what to do to complete the bond. I don't want to hurt her, she might cry, even if we prick a finger."

Anatoli looks at the males that are now leaving the hall back to the barracks on the eastern side, to the pride they fought with and the healers working on them. The attention they had garnered was now on the whining cubs that were barely bleeding and bruised with the fast healing they boasted. "It will have to be enough. We will be able to track her with that at least. Until we figure out what she is to be to us. I've never heard of a pride with a female."

Leonid shakes his head in agreement, "me either. Or a female at all. You said she is different, maybe we will be the first."

"What we did, is that allowed?" Daniil sounds a little unsure even if he went right along with them. He and Josef aren't as far in lessons as Leonid and Anatoli are, so they don't know how much etiquette they just broke. Them following without question is just a testament to the power of their own pride bond.

"No, it isn't. We aren't even to exchange with each other until we are fully mature. And it is supposed to be a bite. The Alpha bites his pride in order of who is what to him. Next, he cuts his arm and we drink from him to seal the bond. We could be in a whole world of trouble for doing it before we are deemed ready, add in she is a girl..." Leonid shifts the baby in his arms, she is getting heavier the longer he holds her.

Anatoli scoops her from him in a move that makes it look like he has done it before, juggling her up and onto his shoulder, bouncing her as he sways. "We used to bite our Alpha back, they stopped for some reason. I saw the bites on Father once and asked him. They are on his arms, two on each."

Josef is peering at the sleeping face next to his own where he is peeking at her on Anatoli's shoulder. "Don't worry, Daniil. They won't know what we did, there is no mark or even a smudge of what we gave her."

Daniil sighs in relief and sags against the wall. His eyes flash with his cat as he looks up at Leonid. "I think I want to bite you when the time comes. Like Father's pride did him."

Leonid smiles at his friend. "Sure. We can do that. I like that idea. Being like Father."

"You're going to be just like him, you know? As soon as we find our fifth. And these two catch up to us." Toli rubs his cheek onto Daniil's head with a chuff for the younger boy.

Leonid cocks his head at that, "what if she is the fifth?"

You're Late

Either her eyes are playing tricks on her or there is light ahead of them. The spot grows brighter and bigger. If it wasn't for Absolem's hand holding hers, she would have been lost long ago.

"You're late." The voice ringing in the gloom startles Katya. He sounds as if he doesn't speak much or is even more ancient than the male leading her now into a room that can only be described as an underground den.

Looking up to see where the light is coming from, it appears that the ceiling isn't there at all for how far away it must be. Nothing but blackness rises above her. Small bugs glowing in a soft gold are scattered around the room, reminding her of the fireflies of summer. Shelves curve up the walls, the books and items on them somehow staying where they are put instead of falling as the frames lean inward. Some of the shelves are built around doors in several sizes. One is so small there is no way any of the beings in this room could fit.

A roundish table is centered on black and white checkerboard floor like the one in the Pale castle. On it is a full tea set up. Cakes and treats of all kinds. A steaming tea pot and assortment of cups. Mixed in are bottles and jars of what appear to be colored flavors and sugars.

"You know I detest being late and those that are supposed to be where they are supposed to arrive being late too. There are plans in the works that you just can't show up to whenever you want. It could throw everything off."

Looking around the room, Katya finally finds the source of the voice, hunched over a desk, nearly hidden behind the mounds of food and drink on the centered table, is a male so old a puff of air might blow him away. As he stands to come around the desk, she sees what she thought was a head of white frizzy hair is actually two large floppy ears he has smoothed back. His movements are shuffling with a little hop. As he turns to pluck something off the shelf behind him, she sees that he in fact has a white fluffy tail at the top of his butt crack. Having been to tea at Haigha's, he is no shock to her. March Hare might be mad, but he and his family are known far across Horunvendush.

Absolem flops down into a plush reading chair, tugging her hand to get her to join him in his lap. The idea of flashing the rabbit in front of her, has Katya holding the vest closed in a fist and perching on the arm instead. "I am where I am when I can be, Rabbit."

With a sniff at them and the pocket watch he pulls from his waistcoat, which is the only article of clothing he is wearing, Rabbit comes around the tea table. "And you brought me a guest. Welcome, Goddess."

Katya jerks back, a puzzled look on her face. The way he said that seemed like a title, not just a greeting. Letting it slide, she offers a greeting back, "pleased to meet you, sir."

She watches as Rabbit makes a cup of tea, splashing what smells like a liberal amount of whiskey in before adding a large spoon of a blue, cream-like substance. With a slurp and lip smack, he gives a shudder and becomes a new male, literally. Time turns back until he is no longer stooped with age, his blue eyes brighten, his ears stand tall, his coat gleams in the low lights. "Now, I know why you are here and you are, in fact, late. You should have been here hours ago. But as that one said," he points a sharp nailed finger at Absolem who had pulled a pipe from his pants pocket and is puffing on it, "we arrive when we are where we are supposed to be. Even if I detest it."

Puffing smoke rings in the direction of where the ceiling should be, Absolem smiles at Katya when she looks at him.

"Now, I understand that you came here today with a babe. A tiny thing, newly come to this world." Katya nods at him when he pauses for her response, how he knows of this seems to be a question for another time. Still pointing at Absolem who was lounging with a leg over the other arm of the chair, he goes on, "and you, you want to know if she is the one."

Flipping open a book that is nearly as thick as one of Aboslem's thighs and now open, nearly as long as the Time Keeper is tall, he straightens a page that looks to have come loose.

Silence has the crackle of the tobacco in the pipe in Aboslem's hand as he draws on it loud.

Shaking his head, Rabbit closes the book gently, making sure that page stays tucked, before setting back in his chair. Elbows on the arms, fingers steepled under his chin, he taps his thumbs against his lips. His nose gives a twitch as he drifts deep into thought.

"For the love of fuck, spit it out would you? It is a simple question." Absolem flings his hands at the white furred male with a growl of frustration.

"Neither question, nor its answer is simple. In answering what you ask, I can influence the future and I am not keen to do so, not again. When the balance could be influenced but the direction unknown, patience is now needed." Rabbit smooths an ear, tugging it down so he can rub a spot on the tip to clean it.

"ARGH! Why do I bother with you? I know. I know the answer. I just needed you to confirm it." Standing over the male that is now polishing his watch case on a handkerchief, Absolem's chest heaved. Smoke, more than if he had smoked a dozen pipes, swirled around the room, engulfing the males.

Katya could hear them talking but it was muffled, her mind drifting as she breathed it in. Those loose pages were the center of the argument her brain was telling her was of no importance to her.

"Goddess."

As quickly as it had filled the room, the blue tinted smoke dissipated along with the brain fog. Eyes darting around the room before meeting Rabbit's, Katya tried to figure out what had just happened. They were talking to her but it still felt smothered. Little sinking in. Taking Absolem's hand, she let him lead her back up.

Katya walks through the door at the back of the sanctuary with more questions than answers. Rabbit knew more than he was willing to tell, that was obvious. Absolem is vibrating with the anger at the dancing around the subject that the Time Keeper had done. If whatever they were referring to could bring about chaos as much as peace, maybe it was for the better that he hadn't told them anything really.

The only bit that was clear, even if she didn't remember hearing it, was that Katya was to keep the child as having girls in Temple was not done, so she was not to be left here. And there were rules.

She was not to set foot in the palace, either of them. As she was the result of a deal, she was to be educated in all things Underland, just like the males were. She was to remain pure until her heat. Once the heat was complete, she was to be brought to him so he could read her. Then, and only then, could he tell Absolem if she was the one, whatever that meant.

The palace thing would be no problem. In all her years, she could count on one hand how many times she had been called there. Teaching her Underlander ways, she had time to figure that out since she was no bigger than a loaf of bread at this point . And keeping a daughter of the priest from mixing with the locals? If she was anything like the boys they raised, that would be a more difficult task than educating her. The simplest task was years in coming, just return her to Rabbit.

"Absolem, I don't think I can do this. As the crone, I'm supposed to be childless. Unfettered. I know nothing of children and the raising of them. Why can't her father take her? Find someone to do as Rabbit said?" Katya stopped in front of her pile of clothes, rubbing her hands over her face before digging her nails into her scalp.

Absolem wrapped his hands around her forearms, pulling her hands down, "my Goddess…"

"And that, you say it like he does. What is that?" Katya looked up into Absolem's face.

Sighing, he pulled her close, directing her arms up on his shoulders where she sunk her hands into his hair. Naked chest to chest. The wraps he wore on his arms were soft but rasped over the skin of her ribs as he wound them around her. "That is what you are. Like I am more than an Underlander, more than bandersnatch. You are more than the Crone, more than the Maiden you were when you first came to me all those years ago. Sadly, the coming of both of us in one lifetime signals a prophecy that neither of us will live to see the end of. And before you can ask, I can't tell you for you cannot change the hands of time as Rabbit would say."

One thing at a time, the babe. Being a reincarnated being would need tabled until she could study that fact later, "regardless, I cannot do this. I cannot mother a babe. I know nothing of how it is done." Forehead to his chest, Katya huffs a breath. The fact the tales of gods and goddesses walking among the people were no longer just that, had her itching to pull her own tombs of lore out. The grimoires left to her had much to say if you know where to look and how to read them.

"Is not the trinity Maiden, Mother, Crone? You are now stepping into the path of the Mother." Combing his fingers through her curls, Absolem watches Katya's eyes slide closed at the pleasure of it.

This male, he seems to have an answer to everything. It is just what she needs when her brain is clouded like it is with doubt to the future. "I was Mother. Mother to all that came into my care before I donned the cloak of Crone. I am ready for my final walk, ready to pass on the knowledge I have like was done for me."

Shaking his head, Absolem gives a tug to the hair in his hand, when Katya looks at him, he smiles into the face of his most beloved. "I know that what you are has not sunk in. You are walking the path of Mother now, it is out of order of how things were done in the past. You speak of an apprentice? She is one. We are meant to live long lives that cross many others, lives that span generations. It is not the teachings of your own crone that have you living the life you have. Ageless, timeless. But this, us, signals we can rest finally. We just have to make it to the end, guide those who are to come after first."

Shoulders drooping, heaving a sigh so large that the creatures in the branches above startle from their perches, she looks into the depths of the eyes that are always just a dream away. "I still think her father should be made to care for her. He could raise her outside Temple. He broke a deal. She was to be a son."

Absolem heaves his own sigh. "I know of every deal brokered. All terms set. The agreements. She is as she should be. It was asked for an heir. Someone to rule kingdoms. Gender was not specified. Greed clouded the deal so the terms were not as specific as they should have been. Was that the fault of the queen? Yes. Should the father have made sure the terms were understood, probably. She is here, she *is* what was asked for. The deal was not broken. Acceptance of the outcome, that has its own consequences."

"Consequences? Even if she had been welcomed, there were consequences?"

"Everyone wants to rule the world. Whether it is a whole kingdom or just their corner of it. Most come to us with the bargain of their bodies or that of someone they can con into giving us what we request as payment. Without the children, we would not be able to save, to work, to protect Underlanders, the old ways. To refuse, to harm, to abandon these children, there are consequences. A deal works both ways. Rabbit would call it the fine print. No one likes to hear what may happen, just what they want to happen."

If that wasn't the most talked around response that Katya had ever heard. She was trying to wrap her brain around it when she remembered her original question and the fact he was avoiding answering it. "But the father?"

"I am the fucking father."

Breath stuttering to a stop in her lungs, Katya took a moment to absorb that statement. She knew the priests made deals, sometimes the warriors. She had never heard of Absolem making them though. "You are?"

Absolem paced away and back. Gathering Katya back in his arms, burying his nose in her hair, he sucked in the scent that clung to her. Cloves and apples mixed with the crisp tones of the winter air she had traveled through to get here clung to her. A hint of rose. "I make deals. Not many. I have to. In an attempt to fulfill my own part of the coming times. I do not want to. If given the choice, I would only welcome one to my bed. She would rule there. Rule me. This babe, a few before her, are mine. I knew not when you and I would be united, but it mattered not. I have a part to play. Forced to play."

Flashes of Rabbit pulling a brobdingnagian of a book from his shelves, opening it to a large parchment that folded out to show something that had made no sense to Katya. Thoughts swirling, it had looked to have been removed from another piece if the ragged ends were a testament. Paper not a match to the ones it was sandwiched between. The markings were not of the language that Katya knew. The images blurry, hard to make out, their appearance of movement making it harder with all that strange smoke. Absolem had growled at a particular place that Rabbit had tapped with that clawed finger. Shortly after, he had shooed them back to the top.

Looking at the male wrapped around her, Katya nodded. She could no more fault him in his past or the part he was to play in something bigger than them. She had a past of her own. Understood long before now that this world was so much more than even them, as a god and goddess, could fathom. Either from the lingering effects of the smoke or just that her brain was in collaboration with her heart on this, she couldn't hold anything against him. Heart singing for the male in her arms and the fact she was being gifted his child, even if she had not birthed it herself, Katya nodded. "I understand. I'll care for your babe as if she were my own. As if she was ours."

That was as close as professing her love for this male as she could get. To do so would only end in heartbreak, she knew this deep down.

His thumb to her plush lower lip popped them open for him to plunder. Panting, Katya gave a little hop. Absolem lifted, arm under her ass as she wrapped those thick thighs around his waist. Reaching between them, Katya found the ties at the center of his pants and tugged the bow. The weight of the linen had them pooling down next to her own clothes and his cock now nudging her core.

Long legs strode to the closest altar where he placed the bounty in his arms on the polished black stone. Absolem, laid her back on it with a hand to her sternum. Fingers curled into claws, he shifted his nails and trailed them down her silky skin, leaving a trail of red welts that had Katya arching off the stone.

Eyes on the male between her thighs, she watched as he tossed his head back and blew out a breath at the ceiling like one does to put out a candle. The room was plunged into deeper shadows, deep enough that when Absolem pushed into her welcoming body, the tattoos on both their bodies glowed.

By the gods, they fucking glowed!

How had she never noticed it before?

"Made for each other. And forbidden to do more than this. What we could do for this world if allowed to do as our bodies want. But no, you are to remain barren and I am forced to seed other wombs." Absolem growled this at her, running his hands down her ribs where every piece of design inked into her skin was a soft shade of blue. The path he took allowed him to hook his arms under her thighs, hitching them up for a deeper angle and allowing her to see that all of her was aglow. Lifting her hands, she watched as the light pulsed as he pulled out and pushed back in. Baring her own teeth at the snarl on his face, Katya moved with him as best she could with him holding her thighs like he was.

Thighs hitched over his hips, Absolem planted his hands on either side of Katya's ribs, powering into her body, his hair curtaining them. She hooked an arm around his neck and pulled herself up, grinding her hips to match his rhythm, planting kisses on his throat. Hand gathering his hair into a fist, pulling his neck back, he couldn't help the snarl as she took a little bit of the control. It was her teeth on his neck that had him roaring to the room.

"You bit me. You fucking bit me." Absolem glared down at the female under him as she smiled and licked the blood from her teeth.

"You said we belonged together, now no one can say otherwise."

With another growl, he pulled out of her body, flipping her over. Her hair fisted in his hand, he arched Katya back to him before shoving in so hard she lifted to her toes. "My turn."

Katya screamed as Absolem sunk his teeth into her. Blood trickled over her collarbone as he clamped down. His barbs sunk into the flesh of her cunt as he flooded her with his cum. Her orgasm causing her legs to give out, shaking as they collapsed. Panting, Katya lay upon the altar, the cold stone cooling her heated flesh. Knowing not to move when the barbs were out, she waited on Absolem to calm.

In all her years and stolen moments with him, never had they been joined. It was from having to treat many who had decided that being with a bandersnatch was worth a try and then freaking out when the barbs sunk in, she knew to stay still.

A purr stuttered to life against her back as Absolem licked the place of his mark. "My Goddess."

***

Echoes bounce off the walls as the doors open to allow Absolem and Katya to leave their sanctuary. To those watching them leave the pristine space of worship, their glamor firmly in place, they are Crone and Father. Mating bites hidden under robes though they throb with the heartbeat of the person next to them, they move with the steps of those far advanced in years.

The pride closest to the door stands with the healers. Their wounds are nearly gone from the treatments, but enough shows that they were well beaten. Before Katya's arrival, the boys had been summoned and been waiting as part of the punishment. Mental warfare was just as important as physical and what better way to learn that then first hand, waiting for judgement to be handed down.

Heads bowed as the pair stopped to handle this first.

"What was decided by their mentor?" Absolem stands tall, the staff in his right hand most would think was to aid him in walking, causing the boys to worry that they were in for a beating with it. The older prides did like to tell stories to scare the younger ones.

Robe rustling on the floor, the alpha of the healer pride that attended them steps forward. "They are to clean the stables for a fortnight, Father."

Nodding at the punishment, he looks to the boys who are now thinking they got off easy. "By themselves. Full stable duties, not just cleaning." Tapping his finger to his temple, Absolem looks each of them in the eyes. They lose their looks of relief. "If I even sense that you are bullying those that are meant to be brothers, even if not in your pride, you will find yourselves removed from Temple. We are strongest together. If we allow hate to grow, we will weaken and when we need each other most, when the enemy is at the gates, we will fall. Leonid's pride will be joining yours in the stable duties, I suggest you figure out how to work it out."

The boys and healers leave with a flick of Absolem's hand. Katya walks to where a pile of clothes is the boys she left the babe with. A pile of limbs surround where she lays on the chest of the boy she entrusted her with. The others surround them to form a cradle to keep the little one safe. Kneeling down, Katya wipes the tawny hair back from the forehead of the boy, "I need to be going, I need the babe."

Leonid wakes, startled. But his arms wrap tighter to the little girl asleep on his chest, she moved not an inch. "Crone. Must you take her?"

Absolem kneels down on one knee and scoops the child from Leonid's arms. Peeling the blankets back, he looks into the face of his daughter. All other children born to him had been male and sadly not survived long as if this world knew to keep them would upset the balance. She was a marvel. "Ah, little one, did you find a protector?"

The boys all scramble to their feet at the sound of Father. "She is ours."

Katya and Absolem share a look before turning back to Anatoli. "Yours? How so?"

Anatoli steps next to Leonid who had been trying to shield his pride mates. "My cat told me."

Nodding, Aboslem stood and handed the little girl to Katya who tucked her into a long shawl she was using as a wrap to bind her to her chest so her hands were free. "Did he now? And then what?"

The boys all exchanged looks. Did he know? Of course he did. Leonid answers, placing a hand on Daniil's shoulder before stepping forward once again. "We marked her. Like pride."

Absolem wasn't shocked but Katya gasped and began searching what she could on the child. Laying a calming hand on her arm before she stripped the child bare in the chill that was hall, he turned back to the boys. "You know the rules. Seems you have more than fighting to be punished for. You know blood sharing is not allowed for those as young as you are. And I know it happens, even with the rules in place. Pride is pride. It is felt deep, soul deep. But she cannot be part of a pride. She is not a male, she is not..."

Absolem trailed off when Anatoli drew up to his full height. Poor cub. Kept from us by a mother who only wanted to love him. Repressing his cat until it died to keep him in her arms longer. Breaking what made him what was. To think that you were less than just because you were different in a world where that was the norm. The words dyed on his tongue. How was he to make these boys understand something that full grown males would have a hard time wrapping their brains around? He could no more tell them of their futures as he could tell Katya of the prophecy. Ever the male that leads by example, he apologized. "I'm sorry. Her not being bandersnatch is not what I was going to say, but I'm sure you thought that was what was going to come out. She is not pride material and let us leave it at that. She will not be able to tug that tether and neither will you. It will not work."

"But it is. I feel her." All eyes went to Daniil. He was rubbing his sternum again.

Katya looked down at the child that was nestled to her chest. It was a wonder that she had not woken to feed yet. "Father," she wouldn't call him anything less than his title in front of his people, "I need to be going. To be home before she wakes."

"As you wish. Safe travels." With a bow and curtsey, they parted ways.

"Crone?"

The small voice of the quietest of the boys stopped her. "Can we know her name?"

Katya looked at Absolem. She had not thought that far ahead, sure she would be leaving the child here. He answered for her, "Devena. She is called Devana."

With perfect courtly bows, the boys signaled their farewells.

Death Of A Goddess

Looking up from where I was pinning the goats up for the night at the sound of a cart, I cursed that I had let my guard down. Lesson number two, always have a weapon. Here I was neglecting it and the first, to always be vigilant. Mother had left well before the morning mists had burnt off having been summoned to the Crimson Court the night before, she wasn't due back until tomorrow so the approaching vehicle had my hackles raised.

Stepping back into the shadows of the barn, I could do no more than wait to see who approached. Many lessons had been drilled into my head not to trust any person, especially when alone. Those lessons were backed up when the local children had bullied me for being the daughter of the Crone, a bastard, and just strange compared to them. Many a wound I had come home with until I learned to defend myself.

"Hello, the house. Devana. You here?" The voice rang across the clearing, startling the goats at the unfamiliar tones.

I would recognize that voice anywhere. For years Leonid's pride had been coming around. But I still couldn't be too welcoming. Traps and snares waited for even those we knew but might have nefarious thoughts. Peeking out a crack between the boards, watching as a group of males emerged on horseback from the evening shadows, one was leading a very familiar horse and cart. Ignoring all the things that Mother had drummed into my head, I rushed from the relative safety of the shed. "Toli? Why do you have Mama's cart?"

The pride dismounted, holding back as Leonid approached where I stood in the yard. "Devana, let's go inside."

Shaking my head, I took a shaky step towards where Daniil held a rope tied to the bridle of the pony. "Tell me."

"The cart was delivered to Temple. Father sent us to bring her back to you." Leonid placed a large hand on my shoulder to keep me in place. "We are to help you prepare her pyre."

"I don't think... I can't..." Looking up at Leonid, the tears came before I could stop them. I had had this feeling since midday, deep down I knew, I just knew, something had happened to Mother.

"Come here, Maiden" Anatoli took me from Leonid as Daniil led the tired pony to the small pen attached to the barn. Wrapping his arms around me, he let me bury my face in his chest where my sniffles were muffled by his shirt. Mother was gone and I was now alone.

The fire blazed well into the night as we returned the body of the only person who loved me to the earth. Images danced among the flames as I stood watching the platform they had built as I had prepared my mother's body. She had looked so frail on the table as I cleansed her, weaving her long hair into her favored braid, twinning in herbs to help aid her crossing.

The wound on her neck was hideous. With shaking fingers I cleaned the dried blood from it before wrapping it with a length of cloth we kept for binding. I had heard the tales of the courts and their penchant to remove heads. I was immensely thankful that they had not done that to her. That her body was returned and not displayed for whatever they had deemed her death payment for. None of the people would have dared harm a hair on her head, it was without a doubt that I knew it was someone from the red queen's employ who had done this. And under that bitch's order without a doubt. Tears splashed her cold flesh as I wrapped her vessel in a length of sheeting, leaving small smudges where they dropped.

Anatoli had come to collect her when I was done. If I thought she was small on the table, it was nothing compared to these males. Bandersnatch were fine specimens of male, far larger than the people of the land. This pride had grown into their forms over the years of our friendship. Toli was the slimmest but still set many hearts a flutter.

He laid her gently on the bed of ferns and herbs I had instructed them to pad the top with. Removing my boots and grounding, I tipped my head back, speaking my prayer to the moon. My voice cracked as the words became the song my heart screamed in mourning. Stepping up to the pyre, I place mother's favored dagger over her crossed hands. With a last stroke of her head, I step back into Anatoli. Josef and Daniil each took one of my hands as Leonid placed the lit torch in his hand in a cavity at the base.

Clouds had long covered the face of the moon and her stars as if it too was in mourning. Embers gave the yard the only light as I sat on the ground watching what was left of my mother was returned to the dust from which we came.

I had done as she taught me in preparation for this day. A day that was not supposed to come for many, many years. In my mind, she would be with me until I myself was ready for an apprentice or if the calling was not of mine, until I had a family of my own. Maybe giving her grandchildren to fill her heart where her own never resided.

One of her many rules was to be prepared for any future. That way when it came, even if the moment broke something in us, we knew what to do.

I had prepared her body as she had instructed while we had done the same for others when asked to help. The pyre was built so tall that I could barely reach the top where she was placed. Inside it was woods and herbs that would aid in crossing back to the realms that spat us into this world of cruel beings. Her final bed was made of plants that had grown around our hut. Upon the lighting, once it was all afire, I had used a little of the art she had taught me to increase the burn. Unlike when others passed, we made sure that there was no bit that could be used against us in the afterlife or those that belonged to us that remained. Even the dagger was gone.

Arms wrapped around my knees, my face was bathed in the glow where it rested on them. I let my eyes unfocus in an attempt to read any messages the world wished to grant me. I needed to know what to do with myself, but they weren't speaking to me.

Steps from the forest, heralded by the silence of the passing of something the night considered more, had me bringing my gaze back to the present. I cared not what came for me. My heart was too heavy to react as one might need to when the unknown came from the dark for you.

Remaining in the trees, I could make out the pride. Deeper shadows with flashing eyes when the moon paused the clouds in her mourning. Coming towards me was not one of the males that made up my small circle. Having never met Absolem, I would still know the priest anywhere. His visage was far larger than the males he commanded. And that was not just his body, it was the power that was felt in his presence.

Bare feet touched the scorched earth on the opposite side of the coals from me. The bottom hem of his robes were dusted in the soot from the drifting blaze that was once a beautiful being. My eyes tracked him as he looked over the burnt oval of space before meeting mine. "Do you know what you want?"

I was sure the tears that silently tracked down my face left trails in the dust of the day I had yet to bathe off as I nodded. "This shall not stand but I know not of how to do that. I don't have the strength to wield the same moment onto those that had no cause to take my mother from me."

Hand motioning from his sleeve, the pride moved to come closer. "They will help you. In teaching or doing it for you. The pride is at your call, no matter the chore needed doing."

Glowing eyes, reflecting the moon as it chose that moment to reappear, were the answers I got to Absolem's decree. "Anything? Even if I wish to learn to fight? To avenge my mother that way?"

A single nod was my answer, "yes, my daughter. Anything. I am gifting you one of my fiercest prides to do with as you wish. Don't abuse it, a wild creature is not to be trifled with."

Robes whispered when he turned, leaving the way he had come.

The Fifth

Hands twisting in the apron I had used in an attempt to protect my clothes from the mess of preparing for the coming winter, I moved to the door and the pounding coming from the thick wooden slab. I had taken up my mother's place in this world and a knock of such urgency could mean only one thing. Pulling the handle, I looked out upon...no one.

Puzzled, I stepped out onto the small porch of the front of the house. Tripping, I caught myself on my hands, shoving a large splinter of wood into my palm. My knees were saved from impact by the crumpled form of a male. I had not noticed him in the low light of the evening as his skin was so dirty and of a color to blend in with the weathered planks that made up the covered front. Naked, not that that bothered me.

Scrambling back, my eyes took in the damage to his back as the light from within showed it. Lashes overlapped each other to leave nothing but a mess of flesh with older scars visible on the edges, telling this was not the first time he was abused. Quickly regaining my feet, I moved to his front which was facing away from me, I assessed what I could see. Face beaten unrecognizable, torso beaten, if the rattle of his breaths were any indication, one arm at a strange angle. Hovering my hands over him in fear of causing him pain before I had to, I took in his legs. His feet were bare, one darkened and I feared the cause of that. There was blood splattered everywhere but I couldn't see where it came from.

I needed help. The male was not human. I would have had to struggle to move a man, maybe asked for help, but a bandersnatch? There was no way and that was obviously what he was just from the amount of space he took up. The pride had returned to Temple like they did every so often. They would of course return but I couldn't wait. And neither could my patient.

Running to where Josef and Danill had been chopping wood, I grabbed the sled that I used to move more than an armful at a time. Pausing back on the porch, I debated which side would cause him the least amount of pain. His breathing needed treatment before I could set to work on his back. The filth covering him and what he may pick up from the only thing I had at my disposal weren't a concern. Bandersnatch never got sick. Placing it close to the male, I wedged it under his side before pushing him where I needed him.

Falling back on my ass, I slammed my hands over my ears at the roar that echoed the clearing. Other than the sound I was sure had busted my ears, he moved not from the sled. Setting my shoulders in determination, I moved to the rope on the front, set my feet and pulled.

I was sweating as I finally got the male turned so I could move him inside. Made to move over snow, the boards gave nearly too much resistance. Heaving breaths, I paused in the door. Night had fully come and the only light I had was from the fire that looked to be needing to be fed in the cool air of autumn. Planting my feet on either side of the doorway, I used the leverage to get him moving in the direction I wanted him. As the sled slipped over the floor and rugs, I kept moving so that I wouldn't have to build up momentum to get going again. Cursing my choice in skirts for my wear of the day, I stumbled yet again over the fabric, landing once again on my ass.

Standing, I pushed at an ache in my lower back before moving to light as many lamps as possible, placing them around him on the floor. As I was prone to do when I was alone, I began talking out loud. "You are a big bastard. Not as big as Leonid or the twins but still a big thing. There is no way I can get you on my table without help. So, you will just have to deal with being tended to on the ground until it arrives."

Nothing. Not a twitch or groan. No sign he was even alive after that roar except for those ragged breaths.

Pulling my kit close, I jumped up to get the hot water I kept always ready. A sad smile graced my lips when I thought of momma in any of the actions she had taught me. Kneeling back next to him, I couldn't help the scream that slipped out when a hand grabbed mine, or the second as the door burst open at the sound.

Large legs and boots filled the edges of my vision as I looked at the copper eyes that spoke of what the male was if I had had any doubt just from his size. Scents of the night, the fur that would have been standing on end if they were in animal form, and what made each of them call to me on another level I refused to acknowledge swirled around with what filled my home calmed me. Placing my other hand over the one that gripped my wrist tight enough I was losing feeling in my fingers, I kept my eyes locked on the predator that lay in front of me. "We won't hurt you. I am a healer. I don't know how you got here but you are in my hut. I need to assess your injuries. Can I do that?"

With a blink, the shine faded to reveal a blend of blue and green irises. A nod was his answer when he attempted to talk and no sound came out. A thick swallow had me reaching for the small wooden cup I had set on the edge of the table. Reaching into my kit, I pulled a bottle of white powder out, pulling the stopper with my teeth. Tapping the bottle on the lip, I added more than I normally would but I had to take into account the male's size. Toli's tattooed hand pulled the cork from my teeth and recapped the powder.

Without realizing what I was doing, I set the liquid to swirling with a thought. We were always careful in the presence of those we didn't know but that didn't occur to me as I watched this male watching me. He felt different. He felt like the pride around me. "This is poppy powder. It will help with the pain. We need to move you. It will be easier for me to work with you on the table."

The flash of copper was back as the male looked at the others surrounding him. An injured predator surrounded by males that could take him out easily should have worried me. Anatoli's purr or the fact the twins were rubbing the center of their chests eased the fear the male on floor would lash out and hurt me for some reason. Something about it just said that there were bigger things working here than me attempting to heal a patient.

Leonid held the male's gaze for the longest before he turned back to me. I lifted his head, tipping the cup against his lips as he drank the whole thing. Nodding again, I moved out of the way as hands reached around to lift the big body up with little effort. With an eye roll at the ease they did that and another push of my hand on the small of my back, I straightened up.

Having helped me before, the pride set my space to rights so I could work. A table at my elbow held my kit, a bowl of hot water was set on the table near the male's head. Clean clothes were piled on the other side. They all stepped back but Anatoli, my assistant as he had the quickest, slenderest hands. When strength was needed, the others would step up, but until then, Toli would be it.

As he was awake, I resumed talking to him so he knew what I was about. "I'm going to clean you up to see what I am working with."

A nod.

Skin a pattern of bruises in all colors of healing. Scars, so many scars, littered his body. Deliberate looking slashes that added to the confirmation this male was more than disciplined, he was tortured. A bandersnatch never had as many marks as this male had. Shifting healed them nearly instantly and then continued changes letting them fade more each time. They only remained if they healed without a shift or were nearly life taking.

Normally, I did the next part only when I was sure no one would see. Asking if those with the ill stepped out and making sure the one needing healed was knocked out. With this male, I felt safe. Just as safe as I did with the pride. I would analyze that and the way they were acting later. I needed my focus right now.

Breathing in and out deeply, I flipped out my hands, brushing my fingers over my palms. Stepping around to his head, I gave my practiced reassuring smile to him as he looked up at me. Closing my eyes, I placed my fingers on his temples and concentrated. The room and males fell away and all I heard was the body beneath my fingers.

Carding gently through his hair, tips drifting over his scalp, I paused over a raised area with crusted blood. Concussed. Over his ears. Drum ruptured, right side. Over his face were many contusions. Nose; broken but healed. Cheekbone, same. Jaw on left; still healing from a break. Two molars missing. Cheek and tongue shredded from either biting or being beaten, possibly both. Down his neck, swelling from strangulation. Windpipe damaged. A pinched nerve in the back.

Stepping to the left, I let my hands guide me in the familiar steps that showed me where healing was needed. Left side. Collar bone broke. Shoulder needing reset. Lower arm broken. Broken fingers, mostly likely from being bent backwards. Shifting the arm, I spread my hands over his ribs. As I thought, several broken, cracked, bruised. They did their job and protected his vitals. Below his ribs was a different story. A large contusion, the size of a boot left damage. A second boot to the hip.

With my hands skimming the skin I could see the trauma that was under the bruises down his leg. Whoever had done this had liked using their feet as most were boot shaped. The discolored foot was thankfully a single broken bone with bruising. Right leg was nearly unmarked except for a large boot stomp on his inner thigh, more than likely aimed for his genitals, but thankfully a miss.

Vital organs were unmarked. Ribs on this side showed old, healed wounds. He must have laid on this side while they took out whatever drove them on his left. Back up to his collar bone showed many healed injuries.

With a palm on the center of his chest, I listened to what his heart and lungs told me. Motioning to turn him with the other, I stepped back while it was done for me. A grunt and hissed 'fuck' told me it was done. Keeping my concentration, I ran my hands over the torn flesh. The male jerked but remained still as I made sure that the slashes were the only injuries. His left kidney would need healing.

Stepping back, I breathed in and out deeply, shook off the feelings I had taken on before opening my eyes. Daniil, Josef, and Leonid were waiting to see if they were needed to turn him back over.

Squatting down next to his face, I held the table to keep my balance, swiping the hair from his face so I could see his eyes. Pain. All they screamed was pain even if he didn't make a sound. "If you can shift, it will be easier. You will heal or at least heal faster. I can take care of whatever the shift won't."

Anatoli's hand came down on top of mine, his finger lacing mine where they rested in the male's hair to hold it back. "He can't. I can smell something...off on him, more than the poppies you gave him. I think he has been dosed with amanita. For us, it isn't toxic but stops shifting. Kills humans as I'm sure Crone taught you."

Leonid growled at that. Stopping a shifter from being what it was was a horrible crime on them. Not illegal if you have the right position in the kingdom though. Amanita was one of the first things taught to all children. Which things to eat in the woods was a lesson taught if you found yourself lost or on lean times and you had better learn it fast. Mushrooms, one of the most prolific sources, had many properties and the wrong one could kill.

"Okay, no shifting. I will have to do this the hard way. This is going to hurt. I don't have anything here strong enough to put you out for it. I can get someone to knock you out but I'm afraid with the head injury, that will do more damage. I can do more poppy."

Copper blinked back to the blue green of his normal eye color followed by a nod.

"Poppies it is. There is no start here in all these injuries. I would like to start on your back. If I can get them packed with some herbs, maybe a poultice, I can dull the pain that will allow me to work on your front. That all depends on you and your ability to draw breath."

Blink, nod.

"This is going to hurt like hell, but I will get them all to help me spread it so it doesn't take as long. We will turn you once I have it done. I'm not going to bandage it, but lay a cloth on it to help hold the spread on."

Nod.

"You let me know if it gets too difficult to breathe. Tap the table."

Nod. Blink back to copper.

I wanted to weep at the only sign his cat was near was that eye color change. To be locked away without your animal... I couldn't even imagine.

***

I was exhausted. The chair woven with rope that mother made for the purpose of watching patients was a gods send. Cradling you in weightlessness as you kept vigil, letting your body rest after all the strength left you when you knew you did the best you could. It was now up to the male if he healed or not. And I myself needed to heal.

I had never dealt with the extent he had come in with. My ability to read someone had never been expended to this point. What little magic I had I infused into all I had given him as aids. It had made no sense to use it on any one part of him as there was just so much damage. My feet were on the bottom corner of the bed with a small quilt over me, I fought the need to close my eyes, counting breaths to help.

Creaking floorboards had never been a thing in my home until the large males of a pride had taken on the task appointed them. Momma and I were slight compared to these big bodies. Leonid ducked into the alcove where a length of sheeting was pulled to give a small amount of privacy. I remained still, eyes open enough I could see what he was up to, but not enough he knew I was watching.

First, he checked on me. Smoothing my hair from my forehead before bending to give me a kiss on my forehead, a soft purr lulling me. Blanket twitching as he made sure I was covered.

Moving around the small space, he checked the male. His arm was splinted, wrapped, and laying on the bed next to him. We had no choice but to lay him on his back, with a soft covering. His breathing was steady with the poppy mix I had dosed him with, allowing the pain to fade so he could heal as well as take normal breathes. I would need to dose him again in a few hours. Bandersnatch burnt through tonics faster than Dush did.

I almost gave away my game when Leonid reached for the male's shoulder to nudge him awake.

Heavy lids from the powder laced water I kept giving him opened with effort.

Voice low so as not to wake me, Leonid knelt down on one knee next to the pallet, "male, I know what you are."

Slow blinks were the only reply.

"You know what we are."

A small, barely there nod.

"I need to help you. My cat, he...he says I need to do this." Leonid lifted his hand to show a dagger before wrapping his fingers around the blade. With a sharp jerk, blood welled from his fist.

Opening his mouth, the male held still as Leonid's blood dripped into his mouth. With a swallow, he sighed, body sinking back into rest.

"Will it work? If he can't shift..." Leonid turned as he made to leave the alcove. The blood no longer dripped as his healing had stepped in to close the wound.

"It will help. My cat said so, to start the bond. Toli's agreed." With a small smile that only lifted a corner of his mouth, he stepped back out. His voice carried back in though, "you need to rest. If you go up to the loft, one of us will sit with him."

Snuggling back into my chair, ignoring the command that was laced under the concern, "who better than his pride to care for him when he is the most vulnerable."

Temple Daughter

I sat on my porch, watching as the male who introduced himself as Toras as soon as his throat healed so he could talk, took on the whole pride. They were all stripped down to their pants, feet bare, weapons of choice in hand, practicing whatever it was they were doing. Leonid was sporting the final bite to complete his pride on his left forearm, above Anatoli's. Still pink in healing as he wouldn't shift until the scar was set.

I had no care to join in this melee, preferring my training to come one or two at a time. Not at all like Toras was doing. He had yet to shift, the mushrooms still in his system preventing it. His skin was the many colors of healing. The skin on his back was layers of scar with the new healing stripes. Bandersnatch were many types of cat. Some had spots or rosettes. The twins were striped as were their cats. Toras was like Leonid, skin an unpatterned expanse or the scars he carried would have ruined his hide marks. He would be a large maned beast when shifted.

An ache in my womb had me hunching over a little. My blood was coming and was making sure I didn't ignore it. Days until the new moon, this pain was not needed to tell me what I already knew. The pain eased and I lifted the length of my hair from my sweaty neck, twisting it, looping strands, before shoving the long metal pins I used to keep it out of my way when working into the thick mass. This cycle was going to be a bitch. With a sigh, I shoved up from my seat on the stair and went to make sure I had enough rags to tend the mess.

Another cramp had me gasping, grabbing the edges of the table where I had been sorting the moss I dried for each bleeding. Breathing deep, I concentrated on pulling air in and out as the pain felt like it was splitting me in two. A feeling of wet between my legs had a groan coming at the timing, I was early but it still needed to be taken care of.

Normally, I took care of this in the privacy of my home. That wasn't going to happen this time. Toras was still sleeping on the pallet in the alcove. I refused to let him join the pride in the barn until I was sure he was fully healed. With his arm still in a splint and a few deeper marks on his back, I was not of the mind to release him from my watchful eye.

Heavy treads signaled I needed to suck it up. Before I could straighten, the door opened and the most delicious smell filled the small space of the main room. A deep breath had the cramp easing. Another allowed me to stand back up.

I should have locked the door behind me. Never was I ever afraid of the pride but the males in front of me were now something else. Flashing eyes, teeth bared, noses in the air, growls rumbling, muscles pumped, stances like they were ready to pounce, cocks tenting the front of their trousers.

Mother had instilled on me that males would come around, wanting me to spread my thighs for them. I was a daughter of Temple. Rare. And something that would be coveted for that alone. By bandersnatch and Dush alike. Upon my birth, I was taken to the priests like all children born of a deal were. They knew not who I would take after with the mixing of bandersnatch, and being female. But they did not know how to care for me and had given her an orphan babe. With me came a list of rules and lessons they wished for me to follow. And I had. Until now.

I knew all about breeding. I was barely into my own cycles when mother took me on birthings, explaining how women got with children. I knew the Dush were nothing like bandersnatch. Dush were more like the humans that were sprinkled into their lines.

The males before me were ruled by their animals and would rut and lock their partner to them by barbs to ensure breeding occurred. In rut, they were more beast than male. Muscles that swelled with each breath of me. The patterns on Josef, Daniil, and Anatoli were more prominent.

This was not a moon cycle. This was the heat mother had warned me may come. I needed the males to leave me. I needed to handle this, somehow. I was presenting as a bandersnatch even if I lacked the animal and other attributes that would have marked me earlier. An anomaly, with little written of except for a page in a long forgotten grimoire.

A sound I never heard before drew me up. The growl and snarl in the air was mine. And it stopped them in their tracks as they were working on fanning out around me, closing in on their prey. Like fuck would I be the scared little rabbit that ran from them.

I was a daughter of Temple. I was their equal. I would bow to no man.

"Out."

Four sets of eyes turned to Leonid who had the audacity to snarl back at me.

"I said get. The fuck. Out."

My roar was nothing like that of one of the males but it was there in the final word of the order they needed to obey. I wanted them nowhere near me.

With a twitch of his head, they left me alone with the pride leader. Pulling himself up from where he faced off against me from the other end of my table, large fists planted on the wooden top, his gaze never left mine. The shine of his animal hiding the rich brown the same shade of my favorite hide blanket I favored in winter.

Snarl morphing into a purr, he stepped around the edge of the table, stalking slowly towards me, waiting to see if I would attack, he came up to me. Large warm hands cupped my jaws, tilting my face up to him. The snarl in my throat only got deeper as he ran his nose up my face from lips to across my hair, where he rubbed his jaw and the gland just under his ear on the top of my head. The fucker just scent marked me.

Before I could do more than rear back to give me space to respond, he was gone.

Those rules I had followed so religiously were going up in smoke like the fire dying in the hearth behind me if the urge to run after him, spreading myself for the taking, was any indication.

***

Three days.

Three days of darkness.

Of heat.

Of need.

A need so crawling it made my skin itch. The burn of the scratches I kept digging into my thighs and arms, chest and neck. To keep my hands busy I kept unbraiding and braiding my hair. Elaborate twists made from many strands to simple ones like I wore to work in.

The new moon was tonight. I could feel the location of the males standing vigil outside. One on each side of the house. Just inside the tree line. Blending into the dark. Only their eyes let me know they were there. And their smell.

Standing in the center of the room, I plucked at the front of the gown I had donned when normal clothes were too much. Nipples hard, the barred piercings in them catching on the fabric. Simple ties on my shoulders would have it pooling at my feet with a tug. Nose in the air, I turned in a circle, picking out the smell of the pride as individuals.

Leonid was all rich sunlight on grass when they cut it for the animals. Breeze clean from a lazy day on the river. Dark cherries, tart on the tongue . All with the dominance of his cat lacing it from the front of the house

Josef and Daniil on either side, smelling similar of forest but each with his own seasonal twist. Like the coats of their cats in warm and cold tones, their scents matched. Daniil a warm, wet earth of rain in the humid heat of high summer. Lightning, the ozone sharpness of the impact. Deep pine like the grove we played in as children. Josef's crisp dirt as it lays waiting for the awakening of spring. The blend of pines and cedar as we brought the boughs inside for yule. Clean, cool air that hurts a little when you breathe it.

Anatoli stood with Toras in the back. Sentinels that moved not an inch from their guard duties. Toras with his dark, deep in the night scent. Temple incense and oils I had smelt on my mother once when she returned. Moss and trees of a deep glen only the gods tread. Stone and iron of the warrior within.

Toli was the one that called me the deepest. His animal was the most like me it seemed. Home. That was all I could use when I searched for the word that described what clung to him. The warmth of his fur in the heat of a hearth. The tendrils of all the herbs and spices that made up my craft. Smoke of my nightly fire. The crisp smell of the linens when I pull them from the line. And under that, a bold note that was the magic of his cat.

Cupping my hands, I took a deep breath to see what I smelled like. The vanilla that was always there came through. Now laced with that was the deep notes of jasmine. Something citrus floated by with sandalwood entwined. These changes were a little frightening as I became...more. And like Toli, there was an undertone of magic. And rose.

Rose was the mark of royalty. Mother had had hints of it around her. When I asked, she would just smile and say that not all queens wore crowns.

A deep breath brought another lung full of the pride now to mix with the lingering notes of myself. Eyes rolling back, I let my head drop back on my shoulders. The loft was a dark cave in the peak of the roof. No moon tonight and the stars couldn't get inside no matter how much I wanted them to.

In the shadows I had taken every blanket and pillow from storage, piling them on the mattress that took up most the space up there. Eyes cutting to the alcove, I shoved the shame at having stolen the bedding that Toras slept on. With a plaintive mew, I turned back to the doors. I needed more. I needed them all.

I had been handling it fine up until about an hour after dark. The cramps were back, a twist in my belly. The ache between my legs would no longer be satisfied with my own fingers. Beads of moisture dripped down my thighs when I wasn't pressing them together, smearing it into my skin.

Mother had prepared me for a heat the best she could as we had no other females to ask. Just that damn page. A footnote in texts that should have been extensive. And it was nothing like what it had said. The writer, some long dead crone, had not even touched on what was happening. So much want. So much pain.

Fingers slid into my latest braid, loosening it from my latest weave. Another mew slipped from me to be answered by a chuff from the front. They could hear me. Had been hearing me. When I got myself off, roars filled the clearing. When I paced, purrs soothed.

Moving to the ladder to my space, I crawled into my nest. A giant swirl of items big enough for us all. Kneeling in the middle, I waited. I could hear pacing, steps coming closer. A trill was the answer I gave when a snarl came from the door.

Leonid led the charge. Prowling forms filled my space. Eyes lifting to find me in the dark where I sat on my knees. My Toli jumped, ignoring the ladder, landing on the small space at the foot of the bed in a crouch. His cat was out to play it would seem with its ears and tail on display. His tail was whipping back and forth in agitation. The rings that were in his ears normally were in the pointed versions on his head.

Hands slipping from my thighs, I planted them in the bedding. Eyes on the male in front of me, I gave a deep arch of my back as I pressed my chest down. Standing to his full height on the only part of the floor of the loft that would allow it, Toli removed the only clothing any of them had been wearing for days, tossing his pants off the edge where they must have hit someone if the growl was any indication.

"Pretty kitty. Such a gorgeous creature. Are you ready to let us have you?" Toli moved into my nest as I pressed my cheek down in answer. "You are, aren't you? We could smell you. Hear you. Practically taste you."

King Takes Queen

Swaying my hips, I waggled my ass at the male behind me. A large hand petted me from neck to ass and down my thigh. Handfuls of the gown pulled the fabric up, the chill of the room causing my skin to break out in goosebumps. The material slid to a stop on my upper back, pooling around me on the bed.

Claws slide back down my back, scratching without breaking skin. I could no sooner stop the arch as I could the breath I let out in a purr. She had been growing in me these last few days. I could feel her calling to them. The spirit resided in me without the being itself it would seem. "Such a good girl. Look at you. This pretty pussy is all on display for me. Wet, ready. Do you want the others to watch? To see you take me for the first time?"

Purrs came from the floor below to remind me we weren't alone. I have a whole pride of males to use. A hand landing in my line of sight and the heat of him across my back had my own purr kicking back up.

"I need words. Before you slip too far, too deep. We need to know how you want this to go." Glancing underneath myself, a cock thicker than any I had ever seen slid between my legs, parting my folds, slicking in the moisture.

My gaze found the male that was bent to get to the same level as me. Toli was a sight. Muscles and veins, tattoos. Those ghostly ears. His smile was pure wonton wickedness and sharp teeth. My brain was all about what it wanted as it and my body were on the same page. And it was greedy. "All of you. Here."

It was a different hand that stroked the hair from my face as Leonid joined us. A finger flicked one of the gauges of moonstone in my lobe like he did when trying to get my attention. "As you wish, my Queen."

Confusion wrinkled my brow at the term of endearment.

"The mate of a pride is a queen should they be blessed to have one. And you will be that. Our Queen." He returned the smile I gave him at being declared their queen, a mate, to have someone to care for and care for me since the loss of my mother.

Toli slid a hand under my chest and lifted me to face the males waiting on the edge of the loft. Knees bracketing my hips, his other hand caressed across my hip before dipping between my legs. The moan he pulled from me drifted across them. Shudders and a range of sound responses told me they liked what they saw. "One more question. Who first?"

Brain, body, and heart didn't care. Toli was already there, ready. Any would do and were just as prepared if their hard cocks were any measurement. And measure I should. All were impressive. But the twins, damn. "You. Him. Them. I don't care."

Leonid looked behind me with a nod. He was giving up his right as leader to let me pick the first one I mentioned.

Toli made to shove me back down, ass up when Leonid stopped him with a final question. "One last thing, You are our queen, our mate. But to take our bites, to give us yours... Do you want that?"

My brain screamed no. I wasn't ready. My heart shouted the opposite. Wanting the promise of a family. The creature writhing under my skin wanted to bare my neck for them all. She had been locked up too long. Silenced until now. But there was enough of me still present to know my brain was right. "I want to, but no. Anything goes but that."

I felt Anatoli behind me nod with his head pressed to mine, along with the others.

Face smashed back into the bedding, Toli held me in place with a hand between my shoulders. Fingers pushed into me, bringing a hiss from my throat. The creature that now resided in me didn't want his fingers. She wanted his cock. Virgin or not, she was ready. And a little angry that I was denying her the marks she wanted to strut around with on display.

Toli growled back, pushing with a firmer hand to keep me pinned.

With the pressure of his cockhead pushing in now instead of his fingers, I released a hiss again. The pain of taking my first male had me wanting to pull away and I tried to do just that. Strength above what I normally had allowed me to fight his hold. Extra hands landed on me, pushing me to hold position as well as allowing Toli to use both hands so he could grip my hips.

A deep breath told me it was Leonid being oh so helpful. My next hiss was aimed at him, letting Anatoli to push farther in, severing the last barrier that made me a virgin. "Such a good girl. Just a little more."

A little more?!

I was already stuffed as full as possible. Tilting my chin up, I made eye contact with Leonid who had the nerve to chuckle. He fucking laughed. At me. Stuffed with more than enough cock. "I changed my mind. I'm good. You all can go back outside."

Several more chuckles rumbled in the loft. Fuckers.

Toli purred. Something inside me relaxed and he pushed the remaining way in. Hips meeting my ass, he gave a little pump. Stars sparked in my brain. Each drag had a whine stirring the males in front of me to want to fix what was wrong. The huff of air as Toli pushed back in had them leaning forward in impatience for their turn.

Friction of his thick length in my clutching pussy, had me pushing back instead of trying to escape. Working with the male behind me, I was fast reaching a height far higher than I ever could on my own. Slipping my fingers over my clit, I pressed and rubbed. The stars began to dance in time with our movements. Growing brighter, closer.

Leonid braced himself on one arm, the other snaking under me, fingers slipping with mine before pushing them out of the way. All I could do now was grip the blanket under me as the males took all the work out of this. Pushing my hips back as Toli surged forward, the world built to this single moment. And those stars, they detonated.

The scream that echoed from my hut and into the valley that I lived in had the birds lifting from the trees even in the dead of the night. Walls clutching Toli so tight he could barely give his final thrusts, had him joining me with a roar. Tail lashing so hard I could see it whip behind him, his roar tapered off to a growl. As I collapsed down, I felt a tug internally. Launching back up to my hands and knees, I hissed a normal sound at the sharp pinch.

"Easy. Just give it a moment. Don't pull, you'll hurt yourself."

My brain knew this. My exhausted body wanted to be away from the thing that was taking the pleasure out of this. My creature, she was all snarls at not being able to get this male away from her now that he had served a purpose and there were more there for her use.

Barbs. Males had barbs. I knew this. Faced with that very real fact, while they were hooked into the most delicate of parts of my body, I still wanted to crawl away. Toli stopped pumping me full of cum, his cock gave a final twitch as he released me.

With a deep breath, I flopped onto my back, looking up at Leonid kneeling above my head and his giant cock. A drip of pearly fluid landed on my cheek. His smile was all teeth as he smeared it into my skin, "my turn."

I lay in a panting, sticky heap in the middle of a pile of males that were just as exhausted as I was. My hips hurt. My pussy swollen. My clit thumping with its own heartbeat. Leonid had folded my knees into my chest before pounding me into the piles of bedding. Josef and Daniil had had me on my hands and knees, taking turns between my mouth and pussy, bringing me to screaming orgasm after orgasm.

Toras was the only one not sleeping. Not taking his turn. Turning from my back from where I was resting with my head on Leonid's chest and my legs thrown over the twins, I crawled towards the male sitting on the edge of my loft. Knees bent, arms looped loosely around them, one hand clasping the other wrist. The sway of my hips had him transfixed.

Coming to a stop in front of Toras, I flashed my teeth. He answered the challenge.

Moving faster than I thought possible, my neck was seized. He didn't squeeze, just let me know he was in charge. Pressing me back, I found myself kneeling, looking up at him over me. His weeping dick right in front of my mouth. Popping open my lips, I licked the cum before it could be wasted.

"They called you such pretty names. But you are just as dirty as we are. And that pussy, such a sloppy mess now that they all have had you. I'd take your ass, but I want my chance to fill you up. To breed you. The cubs you carry will be mine." Toras' eyes flashed in the dark. His animal called to what lived in me.

All while he gave me his speech, I licked and sucked on the cock he presented me. His balls drawing up where I cupped them. With a squeeze, I gave them a tug which rewarded me with a growl. Laving my tongue over the head of his cock, I could feel the bumps of the barbs.

Popping off his twitching flesh, I waited for him to tell me how he wanted me. The hand on my throat gripped as he steered me to face the nest of now awake males. Eyes flashed in the dark letting me know they were more than ready to join in. A press of his free hand in my back had me in the same position I started this night in. Ass up, face down, I waited.

Knees knocked mine wider as he knelt behind me. My only warning was the rub of the head of his cock to part my folds before he was in and seated at the bottom of my channel. A puff of air was all I could get out at being so full, so fast.

Growls filled the air at the rough handling but did little to stop the male behind me. Not liking the angle, Toras wrapped his arm across my ribs, raising me up on my knees. "I'm sorry, I can't..."

His words preceded the pull of his hips to where the head of his cock was all that was in my cunt. With a flex of his hips, all I could do was hold on. Nails sinking into his forearms, I hung there as he used me. The purr in my chest stuttered with each push into my body. The snarl in my ear had me giving him my neck in submission. That was a mistake.

Teeth sunk deep, blood ran down my chest and back as I screamed. My cunt snapping down on the male sinking his barbs in with his teeth. Filling me so full it dripped to the floor between my knees. The room around me disappeared.

Tea With A Rabbit

Snarls and shouts brought me back to myself. The creature that had woken with my heat was sated and purring deep inside me. I had thought it would last much longer, it must have been Toras' bite that brought the cycle to an end.

I was not going to think of the other possibility. I just needed some of my herbs to make sure that didn't take and I would be good. I was not ready for that conversation or possibility. And I was Maiden now with my mother's death. There were certain expectations with that role.

With a languid stretch that pulled all my muscles in a delicious way, I moved to sitting. Looking around, I curled my nose at the mess that was my bed. This was going to take several trips to the river to clean the mix of dried and still sticky fluids.

Edge of the loft showed that the voices were coming from outside as the room below was empty. I wasn't prepared to see the males that were recently all over my body just yet. I needed to be a little more ready for the talk that was going to come. They had declared me their queen, I was aware enough for that to sink in, just like the teeth of the last male I tempted.

Our lives weren't meant to be entangled. They were to serve Temple. I was to serve the people. I loved the thought of having someone, someones. I was going to blame this moment of weakness of the recent loss of my mother. A little bit of a cowardly way out, but I couldn't hold them back. Something told me they were destined for big things.

Washing quickly in the vacant alcove, I donned my favored attire. The fitted trousers slid up finger bruised thighs and when they came to rest in place, my pussy cried out. Too bad, I needed the protection of full coverage to boost my mental shields. Digging through a basket of laundry I forgot to take care of in taking care of Toras, I pulled out my chest foundation garment. Tunic on with banded sleeves, breasts now supported and not on display, I grabbed the hair down my back and started a braid.

A knit cap for my ears from the autumn chill, I grabbed a slice of buttered bread someone had left on their plate as I headed out the back. I would make one of them take care of the mess of a meal that was on my table when we finished talking. Well, depending on how this goes, I might be cleaning it myself.

Josef and Daniil were attempting to hold back Leonid from Toras who stood, feet braced, arms crossed over his chest as the pride leader yelled at him.

Anatoli sat on the steps with a cup of tea and his own bread on his knee. "Your boy is in trouble."

Rolling my eyes at the males in front of me, I took the seat next to Toli. "I'm sure I know why, but want to fill me in?"

Washing down the bite of bread he just took with a gulp of tea, he motioned to Leonid, "After you decided a comatose level nap was needed after being bitten, against your initial wishes I might add, Leonid pulled Toras from the house and attempted to beat the fuck out of him."

I froze with the thick slice of bread in my mouth to look at the male. He was a little rumpled looking, some dirt here and there, but nothing showed he had been fighting. Leonid was just as rumpled but what looked like a bruise and some blood was at the corner of his mouth.

"They didn't get far. Tweedledee and Tweedledum broke it up. Too bad because in any other forum, I would have laid money on that fight." The teacup entered my line of sight and I took it to wash down the bread. "They have been like this for a bit. Leonid hurling insults and the fact, repeatedly, that you said no biting and he bit you. It is rather boring."

Toras gave a twitch as I watched him turn his back on the frothing alpha in front of him.

"Are you listening? Let me go so I can pound some sense into him. He needs reprimanding. He took her choice from her. She didn't want what happened, we all heard her say it. He isn't pride material. What women want matter. They are to be protected, not have their choices ignored. TORAS!"

"Shut the fuck up, someone is out there."

All movement ceased. Leonid stumbled when the twins let him go to examine the woods surrounding us.

"Smells like...prey? A rabbit?" Leonid caught the collar of Toras' shirt as he made to lunge into the trees. The male was a little off after whatever happened to him and you could see his beast riding him, hard. The urge to chase the animal that was too dumb to avoid the creatures that were calling this land home for the moment, and to protect his newly bitten mate, had his eyes flashing and skin turning to golden hide.

It was no normal rabbit that stepped from the woods. This one was well over six feet with his ears adding another two. He moved with the grace of one of the cats in front of him, but with a little hop to his steps. He was lean like Toli but still stacked with muscle. His forest green linen pants were topped with a red and purple pinstripe vest and yellow ascot with a large gold watch chain across his stomach. And he was snow white, not a speck of dirt sullied his fur that looked like velvet.

Sparing a glance with the males that all stood in varying degrees of shock, he moved to stand in front of me. "Hello, little one. We finally meet."

I stood with the mug of tea that Toli had made me in my hand in front of my hearth, a fire warming my backside as the Time Keeper, as he introduced himself, sat at my table, picking over the remains of the brunch Josef and Daniil had put together. Those two thought with their stomachs and the rabbit had no problem with that. And he ate meat.

A large slab of ham was being devoured along with whipped eggs long gone cold. He was on his third pot of tea and not from drinking it. He had the habit of gesturing with his cup and more landed on the table and floor than he drank. The butter had a ring of tea in the bell with crumbs and spices in smears across it. "As I was saying, I knew with the death of your dear mother, you wouldn't know that you were to be returned to Temple after your first heat should it present, so here I am. Though I can scent I am too late."

Scent? Scent! He could smell where we had fucked. Where I had taken each of these males in my nest. My cheeks bloomed with color. Lifting the tea cup in my hand, I attempted to hide my embarrassment.

"Now, introduce me to the male that owns that mate bite you are attempting to hide? He is unfamiliar to me." Another slop of tea, soaking the loaf of bread, indicated from me to the male. Toras stood next to the back door, leaning against the wall with his hands shoved deep into his pockets, a little bit of fear making the whites of his eyes pop against the color of his beast's.

"He is our fifth." Leonid handed the pot of blackberry preserves that the rabbit pointed at to him. He forked up a large gob and smeared it on the top of his ham before swishing the same fork in the teapot in front of him.

"Well that is obvious. You have completed your series of bites. I can say that Absolem was pleased by your choice to bear them on your hide then with just a blood exchange. But who is he? He has to be someone of importance enough to mark...the female."

Toli topped off my mug with his own after the contamination of the teapot on the table, an arched brow at the small pause in that statement. Did the others pick up on that? What had he been going to call me?

Leonid looked over at Toras. "I don't know who he is. But my beast does and he is pride. And the female, as you called her, is our queen. She has a name, Devana, in case you were uninformed."

The abruptness at which the rabbit pointed at me with his cup had his tea splattering nearly to the toes of my boots, "don't you get mouthy with me cub. I know what she is. I know more than you ever will. But I am not all knowing and what I do not know is that male. Now, I can find out the easy way, or..."

"The Hare."

I swear his nose twitched just like a normal rabbit when he turned his full attention on Toras. "What about him?"

"He freed me. Arranged to have me brought here. Said to find you if I made it."

Tea cup filled now to the brim, the rabbit slurped it rudely. "And?"

"He told me to tell you that it was true. Everything you knew and would know was true. He helped me but he helps them. He...he was... DOWN WITH the red queen! OFF WITH HER HEAD!!"

Toras fell to his knees, hands grasping his hair. His shouts against the crimson queen seemed to echo but it was just his whispered rant. Toli moved to his pride mate, wrapping him in his arms. I could see his mouth move as he rocked with the male. I couldn't make out what he said over the mumblings though.

"Well, Haigha did always follow his own path. Seems it has led him to the side that calls itself our enemy." Grabbing the cream, Rabbit mixed a packet of powder he pulled from his waistcoat pocket, turning it a vivid blue before pushing a whole biscuit into the small pitcher, scooping out a hunk with a spoon. "Care to finish what you were saying?"

Leonid flashed the rabbit across from him a hate filled look. "Can't you see that it's all too fresh? If you could see his hide you would know that the wounds are deep. Far deeper than even the maiden can heal."

The rabbit scoffed. His gesture at me again, this time with the biscuit filled spoon, saw the utensil flying my way but missing and hitting Toli who smeared at the nasty mess on his shirt. "Maiden? You all sure fixed that, didn't you? Fucked well and deep I would say."

Leonid made to lunge across the table at the rabbit who just sat back in his chair, slurping his blackberry ham flavored tea. It was Toras that stopped him with his answer to the question.

"He was the one who tortures those the queen doesn't want killed immediately. Every break, every scar, every moment was all inflicted by him."

Setting forward, the rabbit set his cup down in its saucer with a snap of china. "To what purpose? How did they get a hold of you? You should have been brought to Temple at birth or at least at weaning if your mother was willing."

"I was born there. In the Crimson Palace. I wasn't the only one. I don't know what she is doing with us. The only time someone leaves is when they can't be broken and she puts them down. Whatever they are doing isn't working. Even without being raised by the priests, we are loyal to our core." His body rocking, Toras stared without seeing the room around him. He was far more broken than I could heal with my salves and herbs. I could reset a bone but not the mind.

Not The Wrong Alice

"Well?"

The Time Keeper looked up from the large ledger he was scribbling in faster than he could dip his pen in the ink to have the words flowing from him inscribed.

Absolem stood in the door of his burrow. Today was not a good day for the priest. He wore his glamour still. The withered old male and not the vigorous body that he really was. This shell was not sustainable or defendable. Rabbit feared for him.

Not many good days had been had for him since the death of his beloved. He was in heavy mourning and the rabbit could not fault him for that. He remembered his own family from long ago. A family that the ruling factions saw fit to wipe from the world fearing the power they had, wanting it for themselves. After all, rabbit's feet were lucky.

Here was to hoping that the news Absolem sought would bring him some comfort.

"She is her. We have not the wrong Alice this time."

Purity Of Blood

Voices echoed in every room but this one. To eavesdrop in the king's study, a being had to be in the room itself. It was rumored to be spelled. However, Alina had never found any evidence to that fact. It was just a well made room.

Having seen the arrival of Tristan, the crimson king, she had rushed from her rooms knowing that with his arrival this late in the evening, Alaric would only bring him here. Tucking herself into a nook where a bookcase did not quite meet the wall, the space was hidden by the curtains over the windows, she plied the patience she was so good at.

Voices came to her from the open door as the two men made their way. With a smile at her own cleverness, she made sure the curtains hid her as the door opened.

"*When* are you marrying my sister?" Voice laced with a whine, Alaric closed the door behind Tristan.

Tristan went directly to the sideboard and poured a generous drink of the bourbon Alaric favored. "When she produces a living heir."

Stopping on his way to get a glass, Alaric gapped at Tristan's back. "She is to be your whore then, your spawn growing in her with no promise of marriage? Ruining her for anyone else should you fail?"

"Fail? Who says the failure would be mine?" Tristan settled into one of the large chairs in front of the fireplace as if this conversation was of no import to him.

"You do. You admitted that the rumors of a curse are true when we drew up the contracts. That you cannot even produce a child from the lowest of servants." Alaric grabbed the bottle and brought it with him to the other chair, pulling it so he looked at the other man instead of the unlit fire.

With a shrug, Tristan tossed back his drink and held out the glass snifter for more. "My burdens will not affect your sister. Should she be unable to bring life to this world for me, someone will take her. She is of the purest line of White. Sister to the king of the Pale. But I will not shackle myself to a woman that cannot give me an heir. I've done so before and ridding them from my purpose, so that I can do as I'm supposed to for my own kingdom, like you will do for yours, is a bothersome burden. So, I will not be marrying your sister until she can produce me a child."

"Child? Will the sex matter?"

Sighing heavily, Tristan leaned forward with his elbows on his knees, the glass held loose in his long fingers. "No. Due to my circumstance, and the fact my mother has ruled my people without a man by her side, the need for a male is not necessary."

"When? When will she become your queen after she is able to prove that your curse is naught but a rumor that the Crimson people whisper about?"

"Half an annual after the birth."

"Why not immediately?"

Tristan launched to his feet and began pacing, "because I will not have my ceremonies performed on Pale grounds. I will not take a wife on any soil other than that of my kingdom. And to make sure it will survive past birth as well."

"Understood, but..."

With a growl at the whining tone, he turned, "and she will need to provide two more children in the five annuals after that birth or the marriage will end the same as my others."

"You are not looking for a queen but a broodmare!" Alaric jumped up and got into Tristan's space.

Tristan had a couple inches on Alaric and used them to make him back up. "I do not need help ruling my kingdom. I just need a lineage to pass it to and I will not put all my hopes on the shoulders of one child like others in the past. My mother had five children, I am the only survivor. If she had had only one, I would not be here negotiating for the womb of your sister and my kingdom would be in chaos. I will not jeopardize all that my family has worked for."

Alaric spun from where he had paced away, hands in hair, "your family? That is another point I wish to discuss before I consider this ridiculousness."

Arms crossed, Tristan looked down his nose at Alaric, "consider? You and I both know you are going to agree no matter what rumor you heard. You need this alliance. You are overrun with Underlanders, on the verge of losing. You need me and my armies."

Alaric drew up to his full height, poking Tristan in the chest. "I need the armies of the Crimson. You just happen to be controlling them. If they take us, you are next. *You* need us as much as we need you. They will do the same to you and there will be no stopping them from taking over. Restarting what the generations before us worked to end."

Another sigh and Tristan sprawled back into his chair. "Fine. What do you want to know?"

Alaric smirked at having won his argument. "You are not full Crimson, nor Pale. Not full Horunvendush. You are not even mixed with Underlander. You are a halfling, but of those that come from above."

Flopping his head back on the chair, scrubbing his hands over his face, Tristan clarified his lineage. "Yes, my father, and that of all my siblings, was a Wanderer. My mother was told like her mother before her that the only way she was to bring her line into the next generations. We have mixed with them before. It is in our history. Your own has them. Your great-grandmother."

"She was not *my* great-grandmother. She is of Ekaterina's line. A line that will die out because she could not produce the required heir. Much like you." Alaric gave a growl of his own. The line of Alice was a bone of contention for him. It wasn't enough that they were Whites. As pure as they come, generations of breeding ensuring they looked even more like a White than their ancestors. But no royal line could claim that the blood of Alice was mixed in theirs. Not for the lack of trying.

The king of the Pale had tried to marry Alice when she decided to stay but she was already pregnant on her final visit. She had turned him away, refusing to kill her child to suit the whims of a spoiled king. Alice's son, Lewis, later fell for a queen but not of the Pale line. She had led him on, maybe even considering it at one time. Until she was told that only a pure Wanderer would bring her the dynasty she wanted. She had sent out members of her Deck to stalk all the known portals and found one, birthing the current Queen. Lewis had married a Wanderer himself when it was apparent that he was not the love he thought himself to be.

Ekaterina was his only daughter and had attempted to mix her bloodline into that of the royals. The Pales were her target as none from the Crimson could achieve that goal for her or themselves since they were female. Her first husband had been unable to have an heir with her and neither did Alina and Alaric's father when he took the crown upon his brother's death.

Arched brow at Alaric's pouting, Tristan continued to poke at him, "Alice may not be your blood relations, but she will be part of your story thanks to your father thinking with his dick. The people will overlook that fact though."

Glaring at the man across from him, Alaric pouted even deeper. "The people are a fickle bunch and without us will revert back to their heathen ways. I will make sure that the White line continues. I will not be like the monarchs before me. My line will be long and prosper. Without the taint of an Alice."

With yet another sigh, Tristan nestled down into the chair with his drink. "All kingdoms have been cursed. It is in the Oraculum. You will be too once you take a bride. Comes with the crown and power you are only playing at. Let's face it, it is Alina ruling this kingdom and had your father not fallen for the wiles of a queen without a king or a child to rule with, you might have had a chance."

"And to break it?" Alaric didn't sound too hopeful.

Tristan's tone was just as dismal. "That is the question, is it not? The Oraculum has been torn. The Underlanders did not wish for us to know of what it said as it must have pertained to them and how to bring them under our rule. In removing it, they wiped their future from our compendium. Until we retain the missing piece, reassembling the scroll, the only future to be revealed is ours and it is bleak."

Alaric's sigh was the biggest yet, "you may have my sister, if she is agreeable."

"She is." Alina stepped from the shadows as the two men, now into their cups, jumped to their feet, staggering into each other. "She is agreeable. I accept your terms King of the Crimson, I will carry your heir and become your queen."

***

"Do you understand what you have agreed to? Truly understand?"

Alina sat at her vanity, the length of her braid piled in her lap as she tied it off. "I do. I heard it all. I learned my lessons well at the side of our stepmother and I am not one to sit idly by while the men talk. Especially when it involves me."

"You will be a whore, a breeder. No more than the Underlander females in those lunar rituals when the moon is full." Alaric was laying spread eagle on the bed across the room. His bare feet all she could see of him in the mirror.

"I will be the queen of the Crimson."

His head popped up, anger coloring his normally very pale cheeks, "you will be a breeder and nothing more! He does not want a woman to help him rule. You heard him say it."

Tossing her braid over her shoulder, Alina stood and moved towards the bed. "You are just as near thinking as him. How do you think our mothers got to be queens?"

"They became queen when their husbands died. What makes you think you won't die before him?"

Stepping up on the bench at the foot of the bed, Alina slammed her hands on her hips and glared at her brother. "Men often die before women. More so when war is upon us. And my dear brother, you both are about to wage a war on the Underlanders. A people that have been growing in spite of your efforts to curb them."

Rolling his eyes, Alaric dropped his head back down. "You will be queen of nothing if they overtake us. Have you not thought that far ahead?"

Crawling up the bed, Alina looked down at the man who was *still* pouting. "I have, dear brother. I need not be queen of either kingdom when I can be queen of them all."

Eyes a shade more red than the pink of hers stared up at her. "What are you playing at?"

That sweet smile hid so much evil. Alina pushed the hair from Alaric's forehead before pressing a kiss there. "Let me educate you, dearest brother. In war, females are spared. We are what breeds the future. And they will need a queen to rule next to their king and what better way to ensure that I become that, should you two fail, than to be the female of both sides of the Horunvendush that is of the rank in power. The one bred to hold and help rule kingdoms. It would go to getting the conquered to fall in line if one of their own was there for them to look towards for guidance."

Large hand cupping her cheek, Alaric pressed his forehead to hers. "You are reaching too far. With the might of the Crimson, we will win and then these plans will be for naught."

Nuzzling her nose against his, she let her hips settle on his lap, her robe parting for the hand settling on her waist. "I am only ensuring my survival and that of my people, and any children I bear, should the tides of war turn."

With that, their lips met.

Whiter Shade Of Pale

Careful of the mound of my stomach, I checked my saddlebags to make sure I had what I may need to attend to the summons. A certain visitor had distracted me from timing my herbs, allowing growth to secure its place in my womb.

I would be breaking Mother's rule of never going to the kingdoms, but what does one do when summoned by the queen of the Pale? An invitation that was delivered by a contingent of Board. And not just any soldiers but Rooks. She had sent all four captains to see me brought to her.

Who could resist such an imposing escort? I snorted at myself as I pulled up into the saddle. Hard spurs and a jerk of the reins had the lead Rook's horse spinning from where he had sat waiting for me and we were off.

Glancing back at my home, I sent up a small prayer that I would return to see it. Josef stood on the porch. Large arms crossed over the chest I loved to just sprawl across it was so wide. He could no more tell the men that came for me no than I could. Even if the whole pride had been there, they could not have stopped this.

And as I had reasoned with Josef, it was just a summons. I wasn't leaving in cuffs. I would return.

The journey should have taken days but the Rook that mistreated his horse cast a portal just outside the village I lived near. We had no sooner rode through when it snapped closed and we were looking at the Pale Citadel. The stone that made up the spires was so white I had to shield my eyes from the glare of it under the morning sun.

With my hand blocking the glow, I could see not a squared corner in the whole thing. Just grouped together round towers and walls. Arrow slits and paned windows curled up the sides. A moat circled it. As we trotted across the drawbridge, flamingos of the brightest pink took flight from the shallows. The deeper pool was filled with pikes should someone dare to attempt crossing. A poor landed bird was skewered here and there. We rode into a rounded bailey and dismounted.

A small boy came from what smelled of the stables and went to lead away my horse. I leapt forward in fear at not being able to make a fast get away and snatched the reins back from him. With an apologetic smile, I excused my behavior, "sorry about that. I will need him close in the case I need more than my satchel. Please just leave him here."

With a small nod and cut of his eyes, the lad moved to take the destriers the Rooks had ridden. The large horses followed him like puppies where they had fought their riders the whole way. With a delicate sniff, I knew the child was not all Dush. I could smell fur on him.

Opulence. White and gold everything. Even the paintings were in such muted tones that they faded into the decor. The only color that added life to the place was the lines of flamingos that strutted through the halls, going who knows where.

Hallway after room after sets of stairs, finally had the men who had escorted me here leaving me before a set of doors so tall that it would take three of the pride members standing on each others' shoulders to reach the top. Looking around, I saw no one to advise me on what to do so I just knocked.

Not a soul was there when the door opened soundlessly. Peeking in, I saw a woman laying on a chaise with a cloth over her eyes, long blonde hair pooled over the arm and onto the floor. Her form was on display in the tightest of fabrics in a shade of white just above that of her skin. Down her arms and legs and torso, gold wrapped like ivy around a tree. A partial skirt fell from the center of her chest at the bottom of her ribs and down to the floor to mix with her pale locks.

A form to resemble the torso of a person stood just to the side. Swirls of gold formed a high collar around the neck area and down the chest, framing where her breast would be, disappearing around the back. From the shoulders the gold spun out into what resembled antlers, ending in very sharp points. Fabric pooled from just under the front on the left to drape to the floor with a second point attached on the back of the right shoulder. The pale queen wore no crown, it was this shroud that was the symbol of her rank.

Neither the outfit nor the shroud were what had my attention. It was the rounding of her stomach. She looked to be a bit farther along than me, but her willowy frame could make that timeline off. When she shifted on the lounge, I could see that not all her form was covered. Her inner thighs lacked both fabric and gold and if the skirting fell too far to the side, her sex would be on display.

With my eyebrows trying to join my hairline, I set my satchel on the small table with the array of other medical items and equipment already spread there. The soft hush of the leather settling had the cloth being pulled off quickly as the queen sat up. Eyes of the palest pink met my own deep brown ones. "You look nothing like a crone."

With a deep breath to help swallow down the rude comment, I opened the top of my kit. "No. I look nothing like my late mother."

With a sniff, she tossed the rag to the side, not caring where it landed. Rolling her eyes, tiny pale feet meeting the floor, the woman in front of me arranged herself in a pose I was sure she had practiced. Knees together and to the side, ankles together and pointed toes just touching the floor. Shoulders back, spine straight, arms relaxed, hands resting just on her stomach. Her neck looked as stretched as the flamingos I could see out the windows. The tilt of her chin gave her the appearance she was looking down on me even as I stood above her. "I called for the crone, not her apprentice."

Another deep breath in through my nose, I pinched my lips down tight to keep from giving the words that nearly tripped off my tongue. Words I'm sure would have my head as a trophy. She might not be the red queen, but this one was no less apt to take heads if you crossed her. "I apologize for that. My mother passed this spring. I have taken up her mantle of healer. I assure you that I know what I'm doing as I have been by her side, learning all there is to know about healing since I was old enough to walk."

Those pink eyes looked up and down me with a sneer to her pale lips, "well, if you must. Can't have the portal be a waste. But I warn you..."

She let that threat taper off. But for some reason, I wasn't afraid of this girl playing queen. With a nod, I began looking over the table. This must be what they were treating whatever ailed her with. From the variety, I was not able to determine what it was I was brought here for. Boils, diarrhea, constipation, leeches, tubing, scalpels, herbs, a jar of rocks, nausea, headaches, rashes, and so much more. It was all a mashup of nothing and everything. "Can you let me know why you needed my mother?"

Another eye roll met my question. "I am fast losing faith in your abilities if you can't tell from all that." She waved a hand at the table and all that it held. "But since you seem to be lacking in education enough to decipher my ailment from the treatments, I am pregnant and trying to stay that way."

There were at least two herbs here that would counteract that statement and three tools to that effect too. "You use all this?"

"Goodness no. This was what the father of my child's mother brought to me today. She instructed me to have a healer brought in that would know what to do with it all." Movement as elegant as her pet birds, heels not touching the floor, the queen stood and moved to pour herself what looked to be wine from a carafe on a side table. "Let's start with that." I nodded to the drink in her hand, "limit yourself. One a week and only if there has been stress."

"Stress? I'm Queen of the Providence of the Pale, my whole life is stress. Try again."

I watched her down the whole thing before refilling and returning to the couch. "Next, I don't recommend any of this, unless you are having trouble with your bowels, skin, teeth, blood, basically any part of your anatomy. Several items here would cause the child to be aborted."

Shaking her head at me, the look on her face said she didn't believe a word I said. "She wouldn't harm me or this child. It is the heir to the kingdoms. You are mistaken. Maybe what is there is too advanced for your level of healing. I mean, you are the daughter of the crone and what did she use? Mud? Sticks? Berries?"

I had had about enough. And better to leave than lose my head. Picking up my satchel, I turned to go back out the way I had come in.

"Wait, where do you think you are going?" The soft tones were gone, replaced by a screech that rivaled her pink birds.

Bag in one hand, other on my hip, I turned back to the woman that had given up her ethereal act. Feet flat on the floor, dumb look of shock on her face at someone having the audacity to walk out on her, arms hanging limp at her sides. She looked a little more normal at that moment. "Leaving. If you have no call for my services, I have things to do. Other patients that do need the... What was it you called them? Oh, mud, sticks, and berries."

"Let her help you and stop being a brat, Alina." The voice behind me warned that someone else had entered the room. On the arm of a man that looked like a good breeze would blow him away was a woman twisted in all the wrong directions. He settled her in a chair, grabbing the wine from the table and placed it in her bent fingers. "Mother wants to see what the healer says."

With a stomp of her foot, the would-be queen flopped back on her lounge. "Fine. But you need to go, Alaric."

With an arched brow, the man turned from settling a blanket over the old woman's legs. From the top of my braid to where it rested over my shoulder on my breast, his gaze ran over my curves. My pants fit my form, boots to the knee, shirt tucked with a leather harness over to hold the knife I was liberated from after crossing the portal, sleeves folded back to my elbows. With a little start, he took in the rounding of my stomach. Yeah, motherfucker, pregnant and taken.

To prove that point, I tossed off my hood made of the scarf Josef had wound around my neck before allowing me to leave. My bite was on full display now. Setting my bag back down, I waited for someone to say something.

"Your mother, who was she?" The rasp of the voice to my left had me looking at the woman. Everyone knew she had married into the royal line. Burying a husband before taking another that was heir to the throne and his two children. With his death, the title passed to his children, who ruled as a pair instead of a king and his sister.

"The Crone. My mother was Crone. I am Maiden, soon to be Mother. We are the healers of Underland, near Temple."

I received no answer. Those cloudy eyes watched me a little more intently as I moved closer to Alina.

Alaric had sat next to his sister, draping himself over the short arm of the settee. As I leaned forward to reopen my bag, so did he, lifting my braid with a finger to see my neck better. "Is that a mate bite?"

Alina nearly fell off the small couch in her haste to turn from where she was attempting to reach the wine without standing. "A mate bite? As in you belong to those animals?"

Now that got my back up just like talking about my mother did. If they had been here to defend themselves, I would have let it go. No, I don't even think then. "I belong to no one. But I do have a mate and a cub on the way. Is that going to be a problem?"

Alina eased back from me until she remembered that the chaise had no back at the foot. Alaric nestled back into the corner of the arm and partial back, his long arms stretched along the top edge. A smile that said he was enjoying the show on his face.

With a thump of her cane, the former queen brought our attention back to her from our standoff. "There will be no problem. The girl's mother was a healer of the toppest tier and with the added power of having a bandersnatch mate and offspring growing in her, she will suit our needs quite well."

If the body was failing, the mind was not. So I posed my next question to the old woman. "And that would be what? I have still not been informed as to why I was summoned other than to look over a mess of treatments that could cost the life of the child before they save it."

The sound of the doors banking off the walls to either side signaled yet another arrival.

Where Alaric was all pale, thin beauty, this man was all dark ruggedness as was the one that accompanied him. You could see enough resemblance to know they were closely related.

Alaric's choice of pants as tight as his sister's clothes made him look skeletal, even as his tunic gave him some bulk in his torso and shoulders with all the gold adornment. His only saving grace was his angelic, almost too feminine, face.

These two were dressed in red leather armor over pure muscle. Boots to their knees thumped their way towards us. Cloaks as deep red as thick pools of blood told which court they belonged to. Each carried a curved sword on their side. A red helmet sporting a plumed crest of red and white banded feathers of the jubjub bird.

The knave of hearts was only discernible from his king by the lack of sashing across his chest. That splash of black, with the crest of the Crimson Court stitched into where it fastened over his hip. A model of an anatomical heart being stabbed by the same dagger resting in a sheath along his left forearm. "You are here to make sure my child sees the light of day."

As I had looked them over, they returned the favor. Never had I wanted to wear the billowing skirts of feminine preference in favor of my pants than I did when these men entered the room. The mate bite snagged their attention and I was grateful for the fact I removed my scarf. Turning to the patient, I squatted down to clear space on the table.

With little regard for the items that would do little to help anyone, I stacked them on a mirrored tray and then shoved them under the wood top. Laying out what I used on initial examinations of females due to birth a child, I looked up at the woman who had resumed her practiced pose like a bird perched on a limb. A benevolent smile turned to the king as he walked around me to give her a kiss on the forehead.

I nearly missed the cut of her eyes to her brother. "Well then, you look to be due in a few months. So worry the child will be lost is minimal if you take care of yourself. Most are lost much earlier."

"No, I'm not that far along." Another quick cut of eyes at her brother.

Got it. That was on her. I still needed to cover my own ass. The man who did as many beheadings as his mother stood looking down at me from behind his pale counterparts. Raven hair, swarthy skin, black eyes to their whiter shade of pale was kind of eerie and made me wonder what kind of child they would produce. Well, what the queen would have, as I was definitely wondering about the parentage of the child. "If you are sure, many things can contribute to your look of being farther along. The fact you are of such delicate structure the main one. And that can cause the birth to happen earlier too if the child outgrows his space. But don't worry, the body knows when the time is."

"His? You know it is in fact a boy?" the king rested his large hands on the shoulders of the tiny woman. If I knew that bandersnatch had never entered either lines I would have thought him one of the prides. But it was just the frail nature of the woman between us that made him look so large. Too many years of bad breeding could do that to a line.

"No, your majesty, I was using the term loosely. Now, let's get started."

I had never performed this private of an exam with an audience but they refused to leave the room and if the queen had no problem with her bite on display, so be it. For all appearances, the pregnancy was normal. With everyone watching every move I made, I was barely able to read the mother or child. She was due much sooner than she claimed. Again, that was no business of my own.

As I packed my kit, I was aware of how tired I was. My cub was strong and growing quickly, making this job just a little harder. When I was as far as the queen, I was sure it would be much more difficult.

"You should remain the night."

Looking up from making sure I didn't forget anything, I met the eyes of the king of the Pale. He was still sprawled on the chaise. His tunic was now open down his chest. A seductive smile lurked around his lips. No thanks. I preferred males with more meat on their bones. I had a variety waiting for me at home. Josef and Daniil with their powerful forms that might not show muscle but were still strong. The packed flesh of Leonid and Toras. Slim lines of lean muscles of Anatoli.

The reminder of what awaited me at home had me wanting to leave that much faster. Standing, I pressed the ache from my lower back. "No, thank you, sire. I need to return home. Would it be too much to ask if I could portal? The cub wants his bed and father." I was not about to tell them a whole pride claimed me as their queen. Less was more with people who had as much power as these.

The stamp of a cane had me looking down to the woman who had said little the whole time I worked. "At least a meal. A portal takes so much time off the journey that you can at least spare us your time to dine with us. A way for us to say thank you. You set our worries at ease of the heir."

I did not know how to refuse them. My senses were telling me that I needed to leave their presence as soon as possible but to tell them no, I couldn't find a valid enough excuse. With a nod, I stood back as the shroud was placed on the shoulders of Alina by her soon-to-be husband.

The Truth Shall...

I couldn't eat. The spread was huge, more than these people would consume in several meals. And each course seemed to be getting more elaborate. But I couldn't eat.

My stomach was tied in knots as I sat there, every instinct screaming for me to run. I should have walked out like I wanted to when the spoiled little twit sitting at the head of the table insulted my mother and all she taught me. Fighting the urge to rub my neck, swearing I could feel the blade already there, I waited for the end so I could flee.

Kicking from the cub had me rubbing him instead. I needed to get out of here. The large windows in the dining hall showed that the sun was setting. I had promised Josef I would be home by now. My pride would all be there by now. Dinner on the table. Waiting on me. Worrying about me.

Servants entered on soundless feet and began clearing the last course. Desserts were switched out for platters and bowls that were untouched for the most part. I hoped that the staff would be able to eat the leftovers. But knowing these people, probably not.

"So, Maiden, what is it like being mated to a beast?" Alaric was swirling the wine in his goblet from where he sat at his sister's side. The leering look on his face had a shiver dancing down my spine. Wine had flowed freely and he and the others were well on the way to being drunk, including Alina. The only sober being was the little old woman sitting across from me.

Leaning away from the red king, who was intruding on my space the more he drank, I picked at the slice of cake someone had placed before me, looking for a way to answer in the sugar flowers I smashed into the china. "Well, like any other marriage really. Nothing different from any other Underlanders."

That was a mistake. These people weren't Underlanders and the mention of that had several expressions of revolution around the table.

Alina stabbed a cherry in some kind of sauce that had the viscosity of blood and waggled it on her fork at me, dripping onto the pristine white cloth that covered the table. "But aren't they animals? Filthy? Unmannered?"

They were drunk. They are royalty. I kept repeating that over and over like a mantra. "No. In fact, my mate likes caring for me and our home. It is his way of showing how much me and the cub mean to him."

"Birthing a creature. Disgusting." She should be dead with the look I shot across the table at the old woman. Former queen or not, surrounded by royalty or not, I was fast losing my patience with them.

Face masked with a lack of emotion, I gave a trained smile to the old hag across from me, "yes, it will be. All births are a little gross. And he might just have a beast of his own since his father is a bandersnatch."

"Did it hurt?" All eyes were on the red king as he leaned farther into me. I could see Alina glaring at me.

All eyes were on me as they waited for my answer. I had no intention of giving them any more of me and mine than I already had. "I don't believe that is any of your business."

The gleam in Alina's eyes had me sitting back in my chair to get as far from these people as I could. The creature that had been in the back of my mind since my heat raised her head with a snarl at the fear turning my blood to ice. I had fucked up and she had been waiting for it. Probably since before when I had been going to walk out on her.

"Really? A member of a royal family asked you a question. What makes you think you can refuse any of us anything?" That tone was sweet as sugar poorly hiding pure venom underneath.

Lowering my eyes in submission in a move I hoped showed I was at least a little contrite, I apologized, hoping I sounded sincere. "I'm sorry, your majesties."

"Tristan."

My eyes flew up to the dark ones in front of me. He was so close that if we leaned in just a little, our lips would meet. Not wanting to take the chance that it would offend them in any way, I held perfectly still. "Excuse me, your majesty?"

Would making sure that they knew I knew who they were in our roles in life get me out of this? His smile was all teeth as he reached over to tip my chin up a little more. Alina's face was a mask of rage over his shoulder. "My name. I would like for you to say it."

I couldn't take my eyes off Alina and neither could anyone else. Her normally nearly sheer skin was blotched with red and her eyes were protruding. The fork with the cherry on it was forgotten, dripping down her hand making it look blood stained.

A thumb was added to the finger and now my chin was pinched in a very firm grip to get my attention. "Say. It."

"Yes, please do. Say his name." Alina's smile had me wrapping my arms protectively around my stomach.

Flicking my eyes to the ones of pitch that were in front of me and back to those eerie pink ones, I licked my suddenly dry lips before doing once again what I was told. "No, Tristan, it did not hurt."

The clink of silverware on china had me looking at Alaric and his smug face as he watched his sister play with her food. That is what I felt like. Prey. To be eaten. Would she pick big gulps or tiny pieces slowly? "How could that be? That bite left a scar and they have these things on their cocks that rip a cunt apart from the inside."

Not that it was a big secret, but I wondered how he knew bandersnatch anatomy. Pushing that thought away, I gave the king not holding my face my attention. "I don't know about the bite, I don't remember much about it but their barbs don't do any damage if you hold still."

the knave stabbed into that bowl of cherries with a smile of his own at having me in a vulnerable position. My life and that of my child were hanging in the balance. "How could you not remember something that would leave that kind of scar?"

Closing my eyes, I folded my lips into my mouth for a second before turning my attention to him, "I was in heat and it was done in a moment of pure ecstasy."

"So you were cumming?" Tristan had my attention back.

With a deep breath in through my nose, I nodded.

"Heat? Like an animal?" I had forgotten she was here. The dowager sat back in her chair, cup of tea held in front of lips that were curled in disgust.

I had fucked up. They were getting too much information from me. They didn't need to know anything about me or the fact I was not all Underlander. Fear was making breathing difficult. "Yes, ma'am. A heat, like an animal."

A very unlady-like snort accompanied her eye roll. "Underlanders. Disgusting creatures. Mixing with those things. Birthing their spawn. You and your mother treating them with your mud and sticks and berries and *magic*."

She sneered the last word like it was a bad taste in her mouth. But she was waiting for an answer to what I had no clue. I went with simple. "Yes, Dowager."

Ignoring me, she just rambled on. "You go to her to rid yourself of spawn and she can't do as she is told. And then when you birth it, she has the nerve to keep it..."

All eyes were on the old woman talking to her tea cup with a manic gleam in her eye. My brain might be slowed by the influx of my flight, fight, or freeze response, but it was working and putting things together. I knew that Mother wasn't my birth mother. That I was a child left behind at my birthing by a woman who didn't want me because I was a female.

No. No. No.

This was not happening.

The dowager was my mother.

Run Rabbit Run

Resounding silence filled the room as I stood, my chair hitting the checkerboard marble floor with a crack. Tristan nearly fell as his elbow slipped from the table he was leaning so far into my space at the suddenness of my move. "I need to return home. My mate will be worried for me and the cub."

Had they figured out what I did? Skin crawling with the atmosphere of danger ratcheting up in the room, I rubbed my arms to stifle it. My creature stood, pacing from the recesses she had gone to slumber after my heat. I prayed to whatever deity would listen that she remained silent. Any sign I was more would see me speared with those corpses of birds in the moat.

Alina leaned forward, placing her elbow on the table edge, drumming her fingers on her lips.

Feet moving backwards at the cruel look on her face, I backed to the doors open to a garden I was sure I had seen when we rode up. If I was right, I could go out, make a left and be where I left my horse. Timing would be essential. I'd have to make it from the bailey before they lowered the gates or raised the bridge.

I was nearly there when Alina rose to her feet, every bit the queen she was in her bearing. "Really? It is so late, wouldn't it be better for you and your...babe, to rest here and return. I'm sure your *mate* would rather have you safe here than traveling at night."

Braid whipping down my back as I shook my head, I took another step back. Rising as one, the three men at the table turned on me. Tristan held out his hand and when I didn't take it, reset my chair and motioned to it with a bow. "Won't you take your seat again? Alina is right, the night is too far come for you to be traveling in your condition."

Rules of a game should be understood by all before play commences. Neither being told the rules or what the consequences were to be should I lose had me picking the wrong hand to play. Darting to the doors, swift even with added weight of a pregnancy, feet flying over the polished tiles, hand breaking the seal of the sheer curtains that kept the night bugs attracted to the candlelight out before weightlessness caught me with a slamming sensation into what felt like a wall at my back.

Mind reeling from the abrupt stop and backwards pull of someone wrapping arms around my ribcage, I scrambled to break free. Room spinning as I was brought back to the table. Dropped into Tristan's chair at the side of the queen of the Pale, I gasped breaths.

Sipping the bubbling wine that was served with the desserts, Alina popped one of those bloodied cherries into her mouth as she looked me over. "Was that necessary?"

Tristan's hands on my shoulders tightened when I refused to answer her.

"Beasts. Rutting in the woods like animals. Spreading their legs for the filth that spews from that Temple. For what? Promises and answered prayers for paltry things. What was it you wanted that you could not come to your sovereigns and petition for? Hmmm? That mongrel in your belly is payment for what?"

The woman walking into the room put Alina to shame in her bearing. Height as tall as the men and not for the spiked heeled boots that climbed to above her knees. Her dress was a deep red as the cherries Alina had been favoring. Sleeves tight from where they barely kissed her shoulders to her wrists, bodice showing off a figure many a young woman would be envious of. From her hips the skirting fell to the floor behind her in a long sweep, the front snug and only just covering the apex of her thighs.

Thighs that were encased in a black gossamer fabric that covered every other inch of her. If not for her hands, you would not know that she had that same sun kissed skin of her son. Where her face should have been was nothing but a void. Rumors were she was veiled due to a failed youth tonic. Veil was not what I would call what she wore. I had no name for the form fitting cloth over her face. Not a jewel, not a sparkle to take away from the headpiece she wore.

Radiants of gold to mimic the sun framed the void that was her face. As she came closer I was able to see that in all that gold were roses. So many roses that they filled in the whole of the crown from where it sat on her deep red hair to where the tips shot out into dagger like points. The shroud that Alina wore was put to a second place with that monstrosity.

Tristan's hands tightened even more as he smiled at the very late arrival. "Hello, Mother."

Waving a hand at him in dismissal, she shoved Alaric until he stood, pulling Alina with him. Both slunk to the side as the queen kicked Alina's chair, slightly shorter than Alaric's, out of the way before setting the larger one centered at the head of the table.

Hands grasping the fabric of her brother's tunic, Alina let him lead her to a seat next to the dowager. Tristan's hands left my shoulders as he took my vacated seat. Toasting his mother with his own fluted glass of wine, making the bubbles drift to the top with the motion, he downed it in one swallow.

Having been outed from his chair by Alaric, the knave moved to stand just behind the crimson queen. On guard for what, I did not know as they were all a threat to me and not vice versa.

I was startled at the power of the voice from her faceless head. "I asked you a question."

Looking around at the others brought me no reprieve. Swallowing with effort, wrapping my arms around my swollen belly to protect my cub the best I could in this moment, I did as she asked. "I got nothing. I made no deal. I am mated to a bandersnatch warrior."

Veiling that thick should have kept me from feeling anything but the hatred in her eyes still burnt my skin as they raked over me, stopping on the mate mark before making their way to the cub. "Lies. I know what you are. Who you are. You are nothing. A plaything for those depraved monsters that call themselves priests. Where are they now? Where is that pride that has claimed you for their queen? Their vows nothing but words to get you to spread your thighs for them. Where is the priest? His holier than thou platitudes to keep his people safe will not be seeing you here."

Watching that fabric stretch in an inhuman way when the snarl that bubbled up from the depths I kept shoving my beast made her smile turned my stomach.

"Ah, there she is. I was wondering if my spies had it wrong. So you do possess a monster. A female. Interesting. You would think that they would guard you better. What else can you do?" If a queen could slouch, she would be as she settled into the chair.

Her questions ran around my head. One word echoing over and over. Where? A single tear tracked down my cheek.

"No worry, we will figure it out."

A Hand Is Played

Ghosts made more noise than this.

Life had just disappeared.

Even the damn chicken that chased people through the square was missing.

Worry ate at their bones as Leonid and his pride walked Temple's path. Cubs were always playing in the side yard that was now just a dust bowl. Practice could be heard from the woods on the other side on any other day was just silence.

Doors that were as thick as Daniil's waist and as tall as the twins if one stood on the other's shoulders protected the males that called Temple home stood open. Never had they been open to just anyone to enter. Laying his hand on one, Toli nodded to the fact that it wasn't just open, but off its hinge. Damaged as if hit with a blast instead of a knock to gain entry.

Half forms stretched seams as Leonid, Daniil, and Toras shifted.

Before they could step in front of him, Toli pulled his sword and slipped into the hall. Jostling, the pride followed only to stop short before running over their pridemate. Sword limp in his hand, Toli was frozen in place.

Bodies. Warriors, bodies torn to pieces as they defended their home. Priests, robes stained in blood, just as mutilated. Cubs, all ages, behind them. Little bodies gathered in one corner, older ones in the front attempting to protect the younger ones like the priests had them.

"Off with her head. Down with the queen. BLOOD WILL CLEANSE!" Toras roared at the sight of the little ones. His head twitched, his form twisting as he fought a full shift.

"You *will* give it to me. We have followed you without question. Done as you told us time and time again. Ignored as we are slaughtered, picked off. Made those fucking deals. Turning over our cubs to fuel your prophecy riddled propaganda. Forced to live in this place, off the scraps of a village dying as its people sneak away. Why? Because they would rather live under the banner of a crown than that of a male that refuses to help unless taking their cubs and mates."

Toras fell to all fours as his full form won the battle. Large golden paws flexed claws long enough to disembowel with one swipe. His golden coat gave a full shiver as the transformation completed, clothes now tatters around him. The scars he wore as a male were dark marks criss crossing the fur. With a shake of his head, tongue licking canines just a little too long to remain in his mouth, Toras moved towards the voice at the back of the hall.

Daniil motioned with his head between the mane Leonid sported even in half form and the prowling male. Anatoli shrugged at the question as to why the male lacked a mane, following just as silently as those who walked on paws.

The doors at the back of the room hadn't been spared the violation of the hall. Great gouges ran down them, impact marks from the battering ram that lay in the way of them closing. Looking into the inner sanctuary, the males took a moment to assess what needed doing.

Leonid had been inside many times. Normally, the room was awash in light to reflect the time of day outside. The trees and grounds full of life. A putrid fog seeped across the moss, making it blacken. Torches were the only light as Aboslem was held on his knees in the center of a ring of half formed bandersnatches. Cats of all types backed their leader as he demanded a due that was no ones.

Miron remained in male form, pacing as he ranted. Where the ones that followed him were torn up, blood of those they had slaughtered mixing with their own, he was untouched. A weakling. A piece of shit that would let others around him do the work. Like the male that mentored him that they had had the run in with when they blooded Devana into their pride as children.

Leonid had met him in the training ring as pride leaders were meant to do. Cheating was his forte. Calling in his pride when he was beat or using underhanded tactics to claim a win. Miron used his silver tongue to get himself out of trouble. Blaming others for his shortcomings. Or his lack of a powerful cat.

Shorter and even more leaner than Toli, he was one to point out, often and loudly, they didn't pick their cat and if he had been able to choose, he could meet his challengers on more even ground. Refusing to learn how to work with his beast. To listen to it. Use its strengths of speed and agility. As one of the fastest of the cats, he should have been able to use that against his opponents. Instead, he pouted when he was out muscled when he went head to head with the larger built males.

"Hurry the fuck up! I want that rabbit! She said the time keeper would know what my future held. Who the prophecy would call to lead us and she promised I would have her as my queen since my own was taken from me along with my cubs!"

Banging from the back of the room was muffled by the trees that seemed to weep with the destruction of their home and the male that had tended them faithfully. Leonid knew of the second set of doors without ever setting foot between them. Had an inkling of what lay behind. Hair raising on his shoulders and down his back, tail lashing, he made to step in and put a stop to this.

Toli's hand on his arm made him pause as Miron paced towards the back of the room had him pausing at the sight revealed.

Absolem was beaten to hell.

Slashes that were the trademark of Miron ran from collarbone to hip, the bleeding soaking the ground his knees sank into. His face had been pulverised. Clothing ripped to shreds. Left arm cradled against his abdomen with an odd angle that said it was broken. Around him lay strands of his hair where they had hacked it from his skull. Cuts and burns from the sharp edges of knives as they had sheared it.

Still he breathed, laboriously, but breathed and that was a good thing.

Hoping their entrance would pull those at the back from their chore of more destruction, the pride surged into the room with roars of challenge.

All hell broke loose.

They were outnumbered. Miron has built quite the following. Priests and warriors turned on their brothers, meeting them head on. These were the males that murdered their kin. Disregarded all they had been taught about brotherhood. Desecrated their religion with the massacre of priests. Slayed the next generation.

All with the intent to take something none were worthy of. To execute a god, to demand anything of him when it was obvious his life was worthless to those he called his children. Absolem had taken them all in. Raised them to be males worthy of this life he provided. To master their beasts. To protect the people from those that sought to control them for their own gain.

Leonid and Daniil slashed their way through the traitors. Toras was a wrecking ball of fur and teeth, heading to where Absolem tried to drag his beaten body from the fight. Anatoli was a sight to behold as his spectral form flowed from one male to another. No mercy was given. Traitors were never sorry for the wrongs they had done.

Miron and the ones that had been attempting to take the Time Keeper came rushing back. They were too late to help their fallen comrades but that was okay, there was room for bodies at the feet of the pride of males that were hell bent on taking them down. Rage was a powerful fuel.

Chests heaving, wounds healing at a supernatural rate from the adrenaline coursing through them, Leonid and Daniil moved to where Toras was a mountain of cat standing over the fallen figure of Father. Miron was all that was left and now given no choice but to get his hands dirty.

Twin swords flashing in the sputtering fallen torches, he advanced on Toras. "Stand aside. I know who you are. You're one of the crimson queen's pets. Result of her own breeding of bandersnatch. How could you do this? Turning on the woman who made sure that you exist? Let me have him. Let me take his power. I will spare you and that cunt you call a mate."

Snarls so deep in bass they rattled the ground on which they all stood was the only answer he got.

Face pinched, Miron attempted to stare down the big male. "They won't let you keep her. *He* won't let you keep her. We aren't allowed to keep them. Breed them and leave. That is the order. Do you think she will let you keep her? I can see that it happens. I am to lead her suite of diamonds. I have pull. I'll be a captain, a Jack. Might even be made Knave. Then I will have the ear of the king too. And then you can keep her, breed her, fill her with all the cubs you want. All you would have to do is serve under me."

Anatoli materialized behind Miron. Claws at the ready, eyes on Leonid for the command.

"I know what you have been doing with Crone's daughter. I know you all fucked her in her heat. I know she is carrying one of the pride's cubs. I would bet it is yours as you were the only one to mark her." Miron licked his lips as he attempted to edge around the beast to get to Absolem, being met only with pink saliva coated teeth from males he took down to protect. "Wouldn't you like to see your cub grow? To breed more. All you have to do is allow me to take the power I'm owed. Let me rid us of the one that would stop that."

Toras needed not the warning Leonid roared as Miron leaped at him. Taking a slice to the shoulder, he snagged the male from the air, tossing him towards Anatoli.

With that wicked elongated smile of his spectral form, Toli snagged him by the throat, holding him so his kicking feet barely stirred the slimy fog around their ankles. Tsking at the male in his grasp with a hint of a hiss laced in, Toli gave him a shake. "I always disliked you."

Knowing he was about to die, Miron laughed in the face of his death dealer. "You are a freak. I should have put you down long ago. Absolem only protected you out of pity. The poor little cub who was broken before he arrived. I don't know who is more pathetic, you or him." He nodded at Toras behind him as he remained guarding Absolem. "To protect a male that cares not that there are males being tortured in the walls of the Crimson Palace."

Leonid stepped behind Toli with Daniil, both still half shifted. Dead males tell no tales but dying ones often have plenty to say.

"Oh, *you* didn't know? He knew. He knew what she was doing. And he never stopped it. Let all those males suffer, die. I took the news to him when he sent me in. Told him what was being done. That Haigha was helping her. HE KNEW!" With a whimper, he sagged in Toli's grip. "How could he?" Fevered eyes of one who had been twisted by evil accompanied the smile on his bloody mouth, "then she found me. Knew what I was. She could have had me beheaded. But she saw what Absolem didn't. I was a soldier. Meant to lead. She gave me that."

Toli dropped Miron. His knees sinking into the dying moss, the mist wrapping around him. "And what were you to give her in return?"

Cackling laughter echoed around the sanctuary as he threw his head back. "Everything. I told her everything. She already knew of the prophecy, whispered in the kingdoms of a savior are not to be ignored. The missing piece of the Oraculum only confirmed it. Why else take it? But it was me that told her of that babe Crone raised. Of a female born to a priest. It didn't take long to figure out who as none wanted to take that blame. Is it, Father?"

Absolem leaned heavily into the maneless male that had protected him, an old male made older by all the destruction of his beliefs, his people, his Temple.

Sighing at the lack of attention he was getting, Miron went on. "The daughter of the head of the Temple of Underland. What better play to make? A queen if you think about it. And what better to match a queen than a king. And who has an available king? Why, she does. She has a son that needs a bride. A fertile womb. Well, it will be once she removes the weed that grows in it now. Can't have weeds among the roses. Hortensia will save us all."

Toli beat Toras to Miron and ripped out his throat before he could say more. Spew more of the propaganda the red queen had fed him. Natural weapons of claws and teeth were just as deadly in a broken cat.

Royal Flush

Ripples caressed the top of the water as Leonid led Absolem into its depths on one side and Toras still in his beast form on the other. Muscles shifted under his hide as he took small steps in time with the dying male.

There was no stopping it. He was dying. Healing waters could only do so much for a male that had come to the end of his time. Being a god was like that. Hurry up and wait. Wait for everything. Wait for the present to catch the future. Wait for the future to become the past. Wait for love.

Knowing it all and yet not being able to change paths as you saw them twist away from you was harder than the waiting.

The birth of his daughter would be his death. And he was fine with it. He was tired. His reward for all his time would be forever with his goddess.

She was waiting. He could see her. A little mad it had to be this way, scared for her child and all that had yet to come for her, but she was there. Smiling, he let go of the males that had escorted him into the pool he had shown them.

Magic was funny that way. From the outside, this was a place of worship. A place of peace and tranquility. A place of refuge and hope. Built into the front of an ancient tree that had survived the butchering the royals of Horunvendush ordered to build their kingdoms. Living, breathing, protecting the people who at one time were the soul keepers of the faith that lived with the wood, with the land. Her branches spread, entwining with the children she planted around her in the hope that they would be as ancient as her one day. To replace the ones she had lost. Sisters, mothers, grandmothers. Wombs that provided all one needed ripped from this plain to fuel the whims of those that took without giving.

On the inside, it was much bigger than that. That is where the magic came in. Halls stretched to bring the outside in. To feed the power of the protectors that had fought to save the last of the sentinels. Housing a god who taught his people, generation after generation, of the ways Underland once was before the arrival of the Wanderers. Persians from the sands of Cambyses in a thwarted desert crossing. Men fleeing in the forests from those they attempted to conquer called Romans.

Taking in the people of Roanoke where the Horunvendush had let those armies twist who they were into kingdoms of Pale and Crimson. The wanderings of Alice as she blipped in and out of her portals. And those pretty little Romanov princesses that ran from the slaughter by their own people. Time here was different as the lives that resided here and Alice had proved.

"Father?"

Floating on his back, Absolem looked to Leonid standing waist deep in the pool with the large maneless male with him. Oh what a striking pair they made. Alphas. Never had there been two alphas in a pride. Not that Toras was a simple alpha. No, he was a Sigma. They didn't need a pride like other bandersnatch did. It was Devana that brought them together and would continue to bind them. She would need them and they, her.

Daniil and Anatoli stood on the bank, waiting on what would come next.

It would be simple.

He would die.

"I knew. He wasn't wrong. I knew. What he didn't understand was that in this game, you have to see the end and not just the play on the board. Predict your opponent's moves. Sacrifice for the outcome. I'm sorry for the sacrifices I've made but not sorry I made them. Take care of her. She will need a pride of strong males at her side. A king, a whole court."

Sinking beneath the surface, Absolem let the water embrace him.

Leonid surged forward to drag him to the surface when the bubbles began. Small fizzing quickly becoming a roiling boil. Toras' teeth grabbed him by what was left of his shirt and pulled him from the epicenter of the disturbance. Glowing water surged over their heads, pulling them apart.

Toli and Daniil pulled Leonid from the water as he surfaced near them, hacking up what he had swallowed. Fighting his brothers, he tried to return for Toras. The pool was no deeper than where it had stopped at Leonid's waist when they brought Absolem into it. You could see the bottom with how clear it was. Now it churned like a pot forgotten on the fire. Minerals disturbed from the action filling the air with their healing essence.

Toras surfaced with a gasp from where Absolem had sunk. The water was peaceful. The light, gone. No, not gone. Toras was glowing. Runes etched his skin mixed with swirls and patterns between to map them together. As his knees gave out, his pride grabbed him and pulled him to lay on the moss.

Moss that was a vibrant green once more. The trees returned the glow from Toras' skin. Small lights winking in the leaves that rustled with the creatures coming from hiding. The black filth that had swept across the room was now a gentle haze as all settled to sleep.

"Well, that was anticlimactic."

Four sets of eyes took in the Time Keeper as he did that strange hopping walk of his. Eyes of clear blue and fur a sleek velvet were at opposite with the armor he wore. Head cocked to the side, ears twitching in the breeze that dried the males laying at his feet, he turned to the mess in the middle of the room.

"I wanted to strike the flame to his moldy ass but noooo, he had to just disappear and permeate the body of someone else. And who is going to clean this up? I suppose I will have to?" He kicked Miron as he passed. "Worthless runt. If only he set his ambitions into helping his brothers and not himself, he might have been something other than fertilizer. Plants got to eat though. Not that I would feed these him. Might poison them from how rotten he was."

"Um, hello, could you do some explaining?"

Ears drooping with his sigh like his shoulders, Rabbit dropped the leg of one of the fallen males he was dragging to the doors, "what? Can't you figure it out? He told you what to do."

Toli stepped forward when the rest just stood there waiting, "well, yes, but what do we *do*?"

Rolling his eyes, Rabbit resumed removing the bodies from the sanctuary with the help of the mist. Seemed the room was just as eager to clean the mess as he was. "Play the game. Protect your queen. Win."

Leonid led his pride back to Devana's hut, leaving the rabbit to clean the temple for their return. They had attempted to at least give rites to the fallen who had been sacrificed in the hall by males that they once called brothers. He had only shooed them on their way, promising that it would be cleansed in time for the return of the Temple daughter. Ever the cryptic asshole.

"Protect our queen. From an actual queen. A queen with armies and alliances with those with armies." Daniil summed up what they all were thinking.

"Off with her head." Toras might have been granted the title of priest from those waters but it did little to heal his mental traumas it seemed.

Leonid walked a little behind the three. Anger had boiled up at the choice Absolem had made in Toras when he had been there, ever faithful. Now it was just a deep questioning of if not this, then what? What was he supposed to do? What was his part in all this? Protect Devana. Sure, they all would. But what was *he* supposed to do?

Absolem had mentioned a king. But there could only be one and what better choice than that made by a god. Toras would be king. Right? Shaking those thoughts away, he looked at the males in front of him. If he kept on that path, he'd be no better than Miron. No, he would play the game as they were told to do and when it was finished, he would take what he was given and make the best of it. After all, they were all supposed to protect Devana. So that meant they would share her. Like a pride was supposed to do.

As they walked into the yard, it was to find Josef pacing a path in the dirt.

"What are you doing? Where is Devana?" Toli looked to the dark house, no smoke coming from the chimney. No smells of dinner in the evening air. No sounds of welcome from their queen.

Spinning at the sound of his pride's arrival, his face with worry so deep it was going to leave permanent lines, Josef lurched towards Leonid, rushing to get out what was bothering him, it all came out in choppy breaths. "Took her. Had to go. Needed for something. Save us. She'd be back. She isn't."

Daniil pulled Josef off Leonid. The big guy was latched on, seeking comfort in his distress. "Calm down. Deep breath. Now, who took her?"

Josef took a couple deep breaths with his brother. Breaking eye contact, he looked back at the pride leader, "Rooks. Sent by the queen of the Pale. They took her. I followed but they portaled and it closed before I could get through."

Toras roared into the night, the runes on his flesh glowing with his anger. Birds took flight into the pitch black skies, animals cowered from the power as one word raced across the land.

"Devana!"

Queen Takes Pawn

"Interesting who fate makes family. I would say that I always wanted a sister, but that would be a lie. Though Alaric can sometimes be a bit of a diva." Standing with my back straight, shoulders back, chin up, I glared at the spoiled bitch that had me brought to this dank stone cell.

Slime the color of those eclectic limes that were favored at summer teas coated one of the walls from the constant drip of water that was fast driving me insane. Tossed in the corner was what was once a blanket but the putrid smell coming from it and the fact something was living in it, had me giving it a wide berth. Not that I was able to move too much. The chain around my neck let me just touch the walls with my fingertips or reach the bucket that was to be my latrine.

"I wonder if I'm being hospitable enough? Being step siblings must count for something, shouldn't it? Your mother did her best to raise us but by the time Daddy took the throne, we were old enough to not need anyone. Including him. It was most unfortunate that he followed the wrong instructions on that bottle. The label must have been for another as it certainly wasn't meant to be drunk.

"Oh, well. He should have had a tester like we do. Not a drop of anything passes our lips before it is sampled. Can't have a monarchy without rulers, it would topple like a house of cards."

Sighing, I prayed for her monologue to come to an end and she would leave me in peace. Noses curled that far up from distaste might just stay that way if the wearer didn't watch what they did. She had her shroud gathered up in her arm, cradled like an infant, to keep it from the grime that covered the floor.

Stomping like a spoiled child, Alina stopped in front of me at my lack of attention. "She has plans for you. Such grand schemes. But you know what? So do I. And mine are far more important. We can't have a little nobody like you being queen, now can we? No. The role is more suited to someone that was bred for it. Someone groomed from infancy to the position. And I do always get what I want."

Anger was a great way to clear a mind and mine was boiling. Plans? Like fuck. I would not be a pawn for either of them. And if that twisted little speech told me anything, it was that the crimson queen wouldn't like any of this. "I wonder what she would say to your version of hospitality?"

Echoes of boots had Alina slipping on the mask she thought fooled others into thinking she wasn't the nasty thing she was. They called me a monster only to be much worse.

"Your majesty, the queen wishes to speak with you." Filling the small door, the knave of hearts gave a small bow at the delivery of his news.

Looking me up and down, she patted my cheek with her free hand. "Don't worry. You won't be alone for long. I have some friends coming to keep you company."

Jaw aching from the force it took to hold back from biting off her fingers, I gave her nothing. Huffing, Alina made for the door. Leaning into the knave, she pushed up on her toes, pressing her lips to his. Reaching up, she tangled her fingers in the hair on the back of his head before fisting it and pulling him down to her level.

With a sly look my way, she stepped back, the mound of her stomach pressing into him as she looked me over. His hand brushed over the child she carried with reverence that told me I was right earlier, that was his babe. Hand over his, Alina looked to where I had my arms wrapped around my stomach protectively. "Shame, I would have loved a new pet but when a queen makes a demand, it must be met. If I was you, I'd take this time to say my goodbyes."

Body locked up in denial, I pulled in a shaky inhale. I was not so dense to know not what she meant. There was no one here other than my child to say farewells to. They were going to take him. When was the next thought to run rampant. Tears had never burnt before. Looking up at the slit that brought in air and a little bit of light, my scream echoed from the dungeons of Citadel of the Pale.

No sooner than the steps of Alina and the knave faded than the door to my cell was opening once more. The same Rooks that had brought me to the castle filled in, taking up the little room there was. Tucking my fear back, I faced them proudly, a snarl rattling my chest as I bared my teeth.

"Well, we can't have that, now can we?"

Panting, my knees having been kicked out from under me, arms held out to either side with firm hands pressing down on my shoulders, I attempted to avoid the strap of leather that was to muzzle me. Thick fingers wrapped in my hair still did nothing to stop me from snapping my teeth, the sharp points seeking contact with flesh.

I was growling at the male to my left when a fist connected with the side of my face. Lip splitting, dots dancing within my vision, I hung for a moment in the grip of the two men as the third took the opportunity to cinch it behind my head.

"There, that is much better. I don't fancy being part of that menagerie you live if you get those fangs in me. Now be a good girl and I won't pull them to keep as something to remember you by. Make a necklace of them to show I tamed a bandersnatch bitch."

Head lolling back, I glared up at him. My beast was pacing, wanting to get to him. I'd show him that I didn't need teeth to bring him down.

"And that is another matter. Can't have you becoming one of those monsters like the males can." Plucking a wooden case from the inside of his tunic, he extracted a syringe. Tapping the glass vial attached to the needle, we watched the bubbles drift slowly up the thick opaque fluid. Pressing the plunger, he pushed the air out along with a few drops that took their time to drip off. "This is something those red fucks have been working on. Guess they have their uses if they have toys like these. Been working on things like this to subdue those freaks you call mates. Testing it on ones they breed themselves."

Tugging at my bodice until it ripped, he ran his fingers over my mate mark before shoving the needle in the center of it. Voice cracking into silence as I screamed behind the mask when he pushed the contents of the vial in. I was dropped to the floor as my body grew hot, sweat dripping from me before chills shook me hard enough to rattle my teeth. Groggy, brain feeling like it was filled with slush, I reached for my mate's bond. Gone. My creature. Gone. Tether between me and the cub. Gone.

"There, that is better. Now we can have some fun."

I was nothing but pain.

Body broken and bruised. Mind drifting on a layer of madness that was the only comfort in this dank room I was sure would be my grave. Laying on my back, my view of the slit in the wall telling me that it was well into the night of the second day, body jerking as the man between my legs plowed into me.

Curled into the fetal position, I had protected the cub in my womb as they beat me until I was too broken to fight them. It was a silly thought now, but I should have prayed that was all they were going to do. Throat raw, no sound able to show my distress, I felt the child in my womb dying.

My baby. He had tried to live. Such a strong little thing.

The stars stopped moving as whichever one it was finished with a grunt. Cursing when he pulled out, "fuck, she's bleeding. She got blood on me."

A rag, more than likely a piece of my own clothing, was tossed to him. "Relax, she ain't got nothing. They don't get sick."

"What if I become one of them?"

Laughter bounced off the walls as the men stood over me, passing a bottle. "You can't become one, you have to be born one. You listen to too many fairy tales."

"Shame really, she is a fine piece of flesh. I'd love to fuck her when she could fight back. Be worth the scars." A kick impacted with my thigh. Sounds of belts and clothing told me that they were leaving again. Tiny lights winked at me as I prayed they wouldn't come back. That I wouldn't, slipping into the caress of lunacy.

Curled in a ball, I screamed silently as my body forced me to give up my last tie to my pride. I knew I wasn't destined to see them again. My time here would end. You didn't use broken pieces to build a future.

Light spilled into the room when the door to the cell opened. Not caring who or what was coming for me this time, I fought to keep my son. If he would only stay a little longer, he might make it. Early babes survived all the time. My mania clung to that image.

Hands pulled me up to my knees, clothing long gone so it wasn't in the way, I was pressed between the legs of a large male for support on either side of my hips. "Shhh, come on now. You're a healer. You know what needs doing."

Leaning back on the chest of the man that was coaxing me to push, I choked on a sob. His tone coaxed me back to the lucidity that was nothing but agony.

"I'll make sure they don't get him. I promise. But you need to get him out so I can take him home." Soothing strokes were passed from my forehead back my matted hair, a purr that sputtered before fading.

Giving up, I sagged in his arms. My body was doing the work I had been denying it.

"There you go. Push. Let him go. He will be there later when you are ready." Hands pressed on my stomach, pushing with it to expel what was once a life. A life he spoke of like the priests did. Of them coming full circle, coming back when taken too soon. How was a person of the Underland faith in this place?

Sitting against the wall, my pants wadded up and pressed between my legs, I watched as the man wrapped my son in my tunic. If I had even a little bit of me left, I would have been wondering about my helper. One who spoke of the Underland beliefs. Who aided a prisoner. One that promised to keep the tiny life from those that would do horrible things to it. Who performed treasonous acts.

Interesting indeed.

Twenty Seven Squares

Tristan couldn't help the smile as he made his way to Alina's rooms.

His mother had what she had been hunting for years. And if mother was happy, the world was happy. Smile diming as he thought of her other plans, to have him marry and breed the girl. Shuddering at the thought of having to rut that monster, he didn't pay attention until he was well into the room.

Those sounds coming from Alina weren't fake like the ones she gave when he fucked her. No, these were full of passion. Those long pale legs were hugging the hips of the man plowing into her, his own grunts mixing with the slapping of his skin off hers. Grabbing the curtains that gave the scene a dream-like haze, Tristan yanked them from the frame in his haste to see who was defiling the woman he had picked as his queen.

Alaric stopped moving as both sets of pink eyes met his dark ones. No cries of shame, attempts to cover what they had been doing. Just the two on the bed looking at him standing next to it. The mound of Alina's belly drew his attention.

Shaking his head, Tristan fled the room.

***

Keys jangled as the door opened and Alina stepped in. Gone was her shroud. In its place was armor that looked ridiculous with her large belly protruding from it. Pale plates of white leather hugged her body like her choice of clothes had the day I arrived. Having been made when she was obviously not pregnant, it failed to fasten and she was bare from the top of her mound, her breasts barely covered as they spilled into the gap.

A giggle bubbled up.

"Laughter? That is the reaction you give to the queen holding you hostage on the brink of a war that is all your fault?"

Cocking my head like the creature that had failed to wake as of yet, I swallowed back another titter by rolling my lips between my teeth. Sound really did echo badly in this place, it was probably a tactic to get prisoners to cooperate. Face burning from the impact of Alina's hand, I waited for her to go on. She so did like to hear the sound of her own voice.

"Tristan has called off the wedding. Running back to his cunt of a mother, crying of war. Do you know he had the nerve to demand you as his mother's prisoner? Like he held any sway here to begin with. A micro cock with an inferiority complex and title that was no more than a little boy playing in another's shadow."

Standing in the center of my cell, naked, while this little bitch paced around me once again, I waited for her to say or do something that was worth my attention. I knew why Toras was the way he was. How easy someone could break another. How easy a mind could slip into fanaticism.

Tossing the end of the high pony tail off her shoulder, Alina stood once more in front of me. "She had such plans for you. Would you like to know what they were?"

I gave no reply.

Crossing her arms over her chest, tits nearly popping from the stretched leather, Alina droned on, "do you know that you are part of a prophecy?"

What is a veiled message from the future, spoken in whispers, hinting at what is to come, but often unclear until the moment it arrives? Cackling to myself I waited for her to answer my riddle.

"A prophecy?"

I could see myself doubled over in glee that she did it. And I hadn't said a word. Not a hair moved as I watched her from the curtain of hair that covered my face from the earlier slap. My body was still poised from the impact as if someone had paused all motion.

Stomping her boot, Alina moved toward the door before spinning back to me. "You were to be a breeder. Nothing more, nothing less. She may have said that you were to marry Tristan but he picked me. Fucking Underlander trash. Where are those males that claimed you? Where was the male that left that fucking mark for the world to see? Where were they while my Rooks used you? Where were they as you birthed that malformed monster? Where are they now?"

Where?

Where??

WHERE???

***

Having been summoned by the threat of war from the boy who played king, the field was set. Sun glinting off armor of white around him only to be absorbed by the formations of black across the waving grasses. Capes and banners and flags alike snapped in the wind as it picked up.

Battle had a scent. In the beginning it was all metal, leather, animals. During there was sweat, fear, anger, blood. Finally, death.

On this wind came another note. Something he couldn't put his finger on was adding to the fragrance that would be his winning moves to take that fucking prick who dared call him from his throne, before turning on that forest trash and wiping them out with the armies he would steal in his victory. Something that made him shiver in his sun baked gear.

The metallic clank of armor was the first clue that something was going on.

Alaric sat his warhorse, facing the army that was to attempt to take his city as the sound grew in volume to the point he could no longer ignore it. Twisting in the saddle, he searched the columns of men for what was causing the disturbance in the ranks. A parting of the rows showed whatever it was coming towards him. It did not appear to be a threat as the men were silent, letting it pass.

A gasp rose as finally one of his Bishops made to stop the figure that was slowly making the way to him. His hand no sooner laid on it when he fell to the ground. The men closest to them pressed farther away, causing the sound to resemble the pots in the kitchen instead of men in battle.

Measured steps brought me from among the soldiers. Looking not up at the pale king as I passed. My sight was set on the true Underland behind the pieces that were set upon this tapestry that would be death.

I could feel the destruction that my steps were causing. The crunch of grass as it crisped under my bare feet. The poof of ash as I lifted each foot for the next step, it coating me from the knees down. From the height of Alaric's horse he could see that each of my steps had killed the ground where I trod. Good. Let him follow it back to his castle and pray for safety.

I did not know how I got out of that cell. How I got out of the dungeon. My madness had me screaming and rocking on the hard stone floor, clearing when the crisp air outside roused me. The sky above me, grass under and a grated door behind me. I just stood and started walking.

My body was a mass of filth that could not cover what obviously went deeper than the surface. No one could have done to them what was showing for all to see and not have it penetrate deeper than their flesh. Madness was the mind's way of protecting it, securing it for what was to come should the body hold out long enough. Large bruises that could only be from fists, handprints, and even a few boot shaped ones marred the expanse of what was once pristine skin.

Jumping from the saddle, Alaric made to reach for my arm when he was jerked back by a rook. Side eyeing him, I made a mental note of him in the light of day. He appeared shocked. Had he thought me done for? Had he thought I was broken? His voice cracked when he gave reason for laying his hands on his king, "don't. You saw what happened. We can't take the chance that the same will happen to you."

Alaric let his hand fall, doing no more than watching me walk towards that second set of forces. My nudity was not a shock to him. After all, it was his sister that arranged for my quarters and visitors. There was no way he knew not what was happening under those pure halls of white.

It was the sharp intake of breath that told me he might think that his sister had gone too far. Back a mess of welts in all stages it pulled as I moved. Crusts of scabs marked where lashes had broken the skin, I could feel them itching. Some so fresh they oozed watery blood as my body was past the point of bleeding normally. Blood caked my legs; the source had to be obvious. Dried and flaky, along with fresh.

The thunder of hooves drew attention from what was the shell of what I once was into the open space set as a stage for this game.

Tristan galloped out to the middle of what would be their chosen battlefield. Leaping from the saddle, he rushed at me. At one time they had been friends, brothers even. It was only instinct that had Alaric leaping in front of him to stop him from coming in contact with me. "Get off me. Fuck! What have you all done to her?!"

"Tristan, don't. They attempted to stop her and when she was touched, the one who did so fell where he stood."

No response came as I continued to put one foot in front of the other, leaving that trail of ashy ground in my wake.

Gaze taking in every injury, Tristan swallowed, hard. Men of war disgusted by the treatment of a prisoner? How pathetic. Here I was, walking my way to freedom and they couldn't stomach what had been done, on at least Alaric and Alina's orders?

The scuffed scab on my forehead where it had been grated against stone as I was held down throbbed under the too bright light of the sun. One eye was so swollen, it nearly leveled the area from forehead to cheek. I could see out of the other but a red haze told me it was just as damaged. Tears of blood, the tracks of which were dried over the numerous bruises, the split of one cheek, pulled as I attempted to squint against the light. I was sure my jaw was broken as that side moved funnily, kind of hanging there, my lips were nothing but pulp. My ears hadn't been spared either. The stretched lobes were ripped, blood trails came from the interior to trail down my neck and the marks there from the collar and their hands.

Bites that were to mimic what my mate had done to show bonding but lacked the power to do so, leaving nothing but destruction covered my shoulders. The piercings that had

116

decorated my nipples had been ripped out. A brand to match those on the horses of the Pale Providence sat above my left breast, angry and inflamed. Wrists and ankles bore the sign of manacles. In one attempt to get free, I had partially skinned one of my hands. The other was a twisted mess to the elbow. The bones had to be crushed, the swelling and bruising hiding so much of the damage. The mound that was my cub was gone. An empty cavity where it had flourished.

Fear ate at Tristan as he looked back the way I came to the set of footsteps that had killed where my steps were, the path broken by the body of a fallen soldier. His mother had made it clear that I was to be treated with some form of reverence. Locked in a room under guard probably. For me to escape would undermine the plans that were to bring the power of Underland to the control of the Horunvendush. Alina should really learn to shut up. He had every right to be scared. Mommy was going to be angry.

My magic was leaking. Whatever they had done had called forth that part of me that I had feared. The part I had fought hard to lock away. To control and use for good like Mama had taught me.

Shaking off Alaric, Tristan followed as I neared his troops. The men shifted to let me pass, but Tristan stepped in front of me. Not stopping, forcing him to walk backwards, he reached for me once more. The only sign I gave that he was there was a twitch of my fingers.

Every animal on both sides went nuts. Tristan was jerked from my path by his warhorse rearing, the reins of which were looped around his wrist. Rooks, nights, bishops, jacks were thrown as their mounts bucked and reared. Others scrambled from the way of the larger beasts harnessed to the war machines of the Pale as they kicked out, damaging the mechanisms. If I had the mind, I would have marveled at the strength that were those pachyderms the Crimson were known for. Four tusks and armour tough skin, legs thicker than any tree in Underland. Pure marvels now were stomping the men around them.

I walked on. The last rearguard parted and I could see the trees at last.

"M'lady?"

In the whole journey from the cells to this moment, I had not paused. The voice of this man-child drew me up though.

"We are but sheep, please remember that."

Turning to the male, cocking my head, I looked him over. Nothing of remark stood out about him, except for a small coin on the chain he pulled from his tunic collar. With his other he pulled the tie that held his cloak on. Taking it from his shoulders, he offered it to me.

A small dip of my chin brought the boy forward. Careful not to touch my body in any way as he draped it over my battered bones, lifting the hood over hair knotted with all manner of bodily secretions like it was the finest of crowns.

"You are led by barking dogs, kings of their own proclamation, powered by their belief in their god. Their book speaks of wolves in sheep's clothing, tempting the lambs to their own slaughter. Of the sheep being saved by the righteous. Those who can see past the disguise. Lies. For they are the ones who are cloaked. The dogs of war that wish they had power. Mongrels that claim to protect the herd but instead feed off it. But I caution you... Waiting... In the dark... Are beasts. They may don the trappings of sheep, but their nature is never forgotten, and they won't be silenced anymore."

The men standing around us glanced among each other, as if to make sure that they had heard correctly.

Before the darkness that was the wood swallowed me, I paused one last time.

Magic rippled under my skin like smoke, begging for release, to be allowed to show them the might that was now us. To thank them for releasing it. Flinging my head back, arms thrown out to the side, I screamed.

The wave of tainted magic traveled the battlefield, knocking men from their feet. Bleeding from the nose, eyes, and ears. Tristan caught Alaric as he fell and began to jerk and seize. The animals that had been revolting fell dead where they stood. The earth trembled with it.

Clouds covered the sun. Thick, shades of grey and black, roiling. Wind whipped, pushing those that avoided being afflicted as they ran to escape the storm and what I called with it.

The wind carried my cry into the providence. Nothing and no one were spared. The people, animals, buildings from the poorest to the richest shook from the inside, many falling.

The mausoleum that housed the remains of the Whites cracked. The marble trimmings of the elaborate building fell from the tomb, crumbling to nothing but rubble. Dried remains were exposed as they fell from their catacombs. Twisting into a curled position as they too feared what was unleashed.

Into the castle, as it sat like a bloated toad looking over the countryside it moved. Alina gasped as it impacted her.

Healing The Healer

Whispers echo around me as the creature inside me celebrates its awakening. Cackles of glee spill from my throat unbidden, mixed with trills for the mates that I feel closing in on me. Toras is yanking on the bond now that I am free of the Horunvendush. Toes digging into the thick loom of the forest floor, dirt rich with the decay of sheds of the deciduous lifeforms that weave power into my being at each contact.

Gone is the destruction. Pure power fills me, pushing me towards the males I can now smell. Overwhelmed by the scents that make them my home, I stumble when I see the first one darting among the trees. Forgoing the limitations that their male forms hinder them with, they are half shifted. Leaping objects, banking off trees instead of going around, speed that is only equivalent to their full beasts.

Toras is the first to me. Velvet gold fur covers him, soft as he wraps his arms around me. Purr rattling his chest as he buries his nose in my neck, I pull so hard on his neck in return of the embrace that he stutters from lack of oxygen.

Rumbles of affection cocoon me. Hands touching where they can. I shiver as the ghost of Anatoli's tail wraps around my leg. "Let us see her."

Fangs large in his mouth, Leonid's command is a little thick but Toras allows him to pull me from his arms. Surrounded by my males, I look up into faces I had thought to never see again. Feeling the power lent me by Underland leach away, I sway. With a final blink up at my creatures, I let the exhaustion take me.

Rocking from being carried in someone's arms gives me a lulled feeling. Fighting the fatigue, I open my eyes to the thick chest of Josef. One of my gentle giants. I'd know those broken stripes under my cheek anywhere. If I know him, and I do, I'm sure he blames himself for allowing me to leave. For losing me. We can't dwell on that. They will be coming. With a sigh, I resolve to give it until we get wherever we are going. Soft smile gracing my lips, I listen to the males around me, reacquainting myself with the sounds of them.

"She needs healing but where will we take her? *She* is the healer but who heals a healer? Who tends her? Father is gone or..."

Daniil interrupts Leonid's spiral. It must be strange when a leader doesn't readily know what to do. "Father, he had that pool. We will take her there."

"No. What if it takes her too?" I can hear fear in Toras' tone.

What do they mean that Father is gone? The priest in charge of Temple? Gone where? Who or what took him?

Toli looks over Josef's bicep, eyes flashing with his cat. "The pool. He says the pool will heal her."

A quick tilt up of the corners of my mouth is all I can give him as I let the rocking and hum of their voices pull over me like a favored blanket.

Chanting pulls me back to the land of consciousness as we enter Temple. Under the comforting scents that remind me of home with the incense and herbs is blood, death, sadness. Something happened here. In time I will get that answer.

Cloth shifting as priests and warriors alike step from our way. The hall looks so much bigger for some reason. Numbers seem to have decreased. Where are the cubs that are always underfoot? Fear creeps on me. What have I missed? Inside, she rears her head, vowing to protect. Me? Them? I don't understand her quite yet.

Another thing to tell these males.

One story at a time.

Leonid and Daniil open the big doors at the back of the vestibule. These smells are even more home. I loved my hut, the woods that circled me, the river that washed me. But this... This fills a hole I didn't know I had. Tells me I found something I didn't know I was looking for. I can feel the power pulsing. All senses tuning to it.

I want down. Wiggling, I push gently on Josef's chest. We stand on a large stone just inside the doors and I can see piles of clothing against the wall. Creature and beast form alike are not for clothing. All that remains of anything they wore is in tatters. Most bandersnatch go barefoot to remain sure in their steps, but mostly to be prepared for a shift. A cat with boots stuck to his legs can't defend himself properly.

It is more than just needing more clothes. There is something here telling you that barriers are not welcome. Not if they have been outside this sanctuary. Reaching for the tie of the cape I was wrapped in, I tug, knotting it farther. Toli steps back in front of me, frowning at my hands and the abuse they have taken before just cutting the strings with a claw.

Moss as soft as the down of a goose meets my feet as I walk out in front of them. I know they are seeing me for the first time as the cape kept most of me covered when we found each other. Not wanting to see their faces, I continue into this world that sighs my name, greeting me.

Gentle breezes push my hair. Small animals and birds stop to peer at me. A fox walks out to keep pace with me before quickening to show me a path. Not questioning it, I step off the moss. Sand sinks around my feet as I take notice of a glow off to my right.

Minerals fill the mist that swirls off the top of the water. Green at the edges, deepening to a blue at the middle, resembling Toras' eyes, the pool seems to pulse. The steam beckoning me in. Fingers wrap the wrist of the skinned hand, stopping me with a gentle tug.

Toras stands there behind me. He isn't looking at me. Fear fills his eyes as he looks at the water.

Dipping my head so I can see him out of my less damaged eye, I move my head to indicate the water.

A quick deep breath, fingers tightening, he joins me as I walk in.

Movement is slow, like wading in oil. Looking down, I can still see the bottom, still see my feet. Pulses of deeper shades radiate from me with the ripples our movements have disturbed on the surface. Thickening, the water wraps around us.

Standing in the center, fluid level at our chests, I turn back to the shore. Josef is leaning on Daniil. The pain of looking at me, at the blame he is heaping on himself plain on his face. Daniil has his arm wrapped around his brother, head on the one resting on his shoulder, mouth moving as he whispers. I know he is trying to reassure Josef. Glowing ripples of light dance over them, making their stripes stand out, seeming to move with the reflections of the water.

Leonid stands there like the king he is. Feet planted, arms crossed over his chest. Twitching skin tells me he is close to a shift. Anger rolls off him as he takes in the brand on my chest. His normally short hair is nearly a mane as he fights to maintain control.

Toli crouches next to him. Hands dangling between his knees, elbows planted on his thighs, he watches me with those cheshire eyes. Ears full of piercings stick up from his hair. A ghostly tail lays around his feet, the tip flipping. That oversized, toothy smile of his cat flashes at me.

Toras cups my cheek, bringing me back to him. I'd brush the hair from his forehead but my hands are useless. Thumb dragging on my cheek, just below the split. A tear runs down his face as he takes in the marks marring his bond bite. The hand on my cheek moves to where the mound of the cub was. Gently he sets his head against mine. A shudder racks his frame.

Purring, I tuck up to him as best I can before stepping back and ducking beneath the pool. I don't have to try to sink or float. It holds me, reminding me of the cloth swaddle swing of my youth Mama made me from one of her old sheets. My only tether to the surface is the hand around my wrist that refuses to let go.

My heart thumps in my ears as I just be. There is no need for breath. No fear making me want to search for up. Sinking, soaking. It all just goes away. A brushing of my hair back from my face has me opening my eyes. Fatherly affection trickles in as does the healing.

Feeling sleep slipping up on me again, I nestle in.

If these males don't stop waking me, I'm going to kick all their asses. Eyes cracking open, I take in my new surroundings. Laying on a bed far too comfortable to be my own, a comforter of velvet and silk pieces is spiraled around me with the corner flopped over my hip to give me a touch of modesty, I sigh at being awake yet again.

"I will not answer anything from someone who does not know how to ask. Try again." Rabbit correcting the huffing giant form of Leonid has me smiling.

"How about I rip those ears off and roast you on a spit, you pain in my ass?" Toli is lounging in a chair, one leg over arm swinging as he attempts to hide his laugh in a cup of tea. Leonid snarls at him but gives what the fluffy persona in front of him was asking for. "Please."

Making a show of having not heard him, Rabbit polishes his glasses before slipping them into a vest pocket. "What was that?"

Eyes moving I look for the other three. Daniil and Toras are sitting on a small sofa, cups of tea in hand, plates of treats piled high between them. Josef is sitting on the floor, head on his brother's thigh as he sleeps, a drool spot wetting the fabric of Daniil's pants.

Leonid stretches, pushing back his creature. "Please, help us."

Waving a hand, Rabbit flops down on the end of the bed, reclining back on an elbow, reaching up to poke me in the nose. "When Devana is ready. How you feeling, Goddess?"

Movement blurs around the bed as the males scramble to surround me. Nudity may be alright with them, but I'm not about parading in front of others I don't have a bond with. Keeping an arm over my breasts, I sit up, pulling the blanket with me. Covered, I turn my attention to the white rabbit sitting cross legged now in front of me. His blue blue eyes take me in as his nose gives a twitch. No need to beat around the bush with him, I let the corner of my lips curl with my answer. "Powerful."

"Atta girl."

Into The Rabbit Hole

"You need to start talking rabbit." Leonid's demand is met with an eye roll. Cheeky bastard.

"And get off the gods damned bed with my mate." Toras makes a swipe at the rabbit that has flopped onto his back with his head in my lap. I can't help reaching a finger out and stroking his ear just to see if it is as soft as it looks, making him shudder and a foot twitch like it was going to thump.

"Rub them. Please." Tacking on the last word softened the request. Toras grabbed Rabbit's ankle and gave a tug before Toli stopped him. All eyes were on me as I stroked those long ears with one hand and the other pointing at Toras. My face said what I didn't have to as he let go of the male in my lap.

"What do you want to know first?" It was obvious he was playing with them as they watched what I was just noticing.

Turning my palm up to examine the underside of my arm, under the skin smoke ripples danced. One would think I had tattoos like many of the males in the burrow with us if they weren't animated. Twisting, swirling before fading away.

Toras flipped Rabbit's big toe. "Owww. I'm not going to tell you anything if you don't stop being mean."

Sighing, I shot the bandersnatch that was pouting the same look my mom used to give me when I just needed to suck it up and behave for a little longer.

"Mmmm, that is nice." My thumb was now petting from the tip of Rabbit's nose, up the bridge, before alternating fanning over each eyebrow. Toras growled low. "Easy big guy, I'm not interested in your mate. I prefer my partners to have more than a set of holes if you get my meaning."

Choked laughter filled the room. Shaking my head, I scratched at the bottom of each side of his ears and this time did get a foot thump.

Throwing his hands up, Leonid motioned for them all to settle back around the room. As they made themselves comfortable, I let my gaze wander.

Clocks covered the wall with the door but by some magic the ticking was silent. A large fireplace blazed away to my right and a buffet table of a tea spread was on the left. Josef jumped to his feet and made me a plate and cup, setting them on a book he plucked from the nightstand. Two chairs used to face the fireplace but the males had turned them towards the bed to keep vigil. A sofa sat across the corner on the other side of the door. Everything was mismatched but worked. Including the giant gauzy curtained canopied bed I was holding court in the middle of with a rabbit enjoying his scratches.

"Let's start at the beginning." Arranging himself so I could reach as much of him as possible, Rabbit began. Grumbles from the audience have him raising his head and giving them a stink eye before flopping back into my lap, nearly earning him a tea bath from the cup I just picked up. "If you don't want me to tell you what I know, you have every right to walk right out of here."

Sighs and the creaking of furniture is their answer. With a dramatic clearing of his throat, the Time Keeper begins.

"Absolem was old when I was born. He was old when this world was in its infancy. I know not where he came from, never asked, he never volunteered. If you don't know already, he was a god. Of what, no clue. No clue. He had a mate who was not immortal. Fated to find him again and again just as her time was running out. He had a pride when the bandersnatch came to be. They were the ones who began the Temple of Underland.

"They were all about living with the land. Peace and harmony and all that shit. And they did it for a time. Ignored by the Horunvendush that lived in the valley unless needing prayers answered. Everyone knew about the portals. Wanderers came, Wanderers went. Our people never crossed, they couldn't. Until I was born."

Toli spoke from where he had his head back, looking at the ceiling instead of the room. "What other Wanderers? There was more than Alice?"

Huffing at the interruption, Rabbit went on as if Toli hadn't spoken. Rude ass.

"As far as I know, I'm the only being from Underland to ever go topside. I don't know how I do it and I didn't go often up there. Time is different and it does something to me each time. Ages me. Makes me age here. My tonics counteract it. I haven't been since the time Alice followed me though.

"She was the fifth. She caused a rift in our timeline as she was able to cross back and forth many times, a first for a Wanderer. When I was named Time Keeper after I was able to escape the service of the queen of Hearts with Alice's help, I wrote it all down. Keeping a compendium of my own. Everything everyone remembered, what I remembered, what others came to tell me. I read all that the others before me had recorded.

"They told of large groups of Wanderers that never left. An army from the sands of Overland. Persians they called themselves. Crossing a desert on the whims of their king. They were dying when a large group of them were sucked into a warren hole. Next was a Roman contingent. Battling a horde in a forest, getting their asses handed to them, survivors took refuge in a cave. Oops, watch your step and here they landed. Both were taken in my Horunvendush. The Persians by the Pale and Romans by Crimson. Giving them more power in Underland than they needed. Thoughts of being more, being better than the natives that were here first."

"The Oraculum that the Horunvendush have does the same, just not as in depth and with a twist. It speaks of the past, present, and on a good day, the future. Time is like water. It flows, changes paths, changes the landscape. No future is written in stone until the present. I couldn't get the queen of Hearts to see that when I was enslaved to her. She only saw what she wanted, doing all she could to make it happen. She even refused to stop her own beheading as it meant her daughter would one day later rule. And a united Underland with one queen after her death.

"Alice had come back for a visit around that time. She worked with the royals of the Pale to remove the queen from her throne, taking her head with the Vorpal sword herself after defeating the polluted version the queen had made of the Jabberwocky. Fitting since she was the one to start the beheading shit.

"Upon its death, the Jabberwocky made a prediction before the head died. It reinforced the Oraculum's prediction of an Underland with a single ruler. 'In blackened black she stand. A crown of bones on her head. Queen of all of Underland. Blood of god and lines long dead.' A poet he was not."

Rabbit patted my knee before bounding from the bed and into the chamber beyond. Rustling and a loud thump accompanied by a 'fuck' and he was back, with a limp. "That sword, it will slice through anything. Even things deemed indestructible."

Leaning forward, we all watched as he took a silk sleeve from a roll of parchment smelling of magic and blood. Spreading it on the end of the bed, he presented it to us with a flourish. "the red queen, sister to the queen of the Pale and Queen of Hearts, took before the blood was absorbed into the dirt. She offered me the same position as her sister held me in but as a free creature. She gave me that night to think of it. Having had enough of all of them, I picked no and fled while they slept.

"Before leaving I took a couple keepsakes. This is the section of the Oraculum with the prophecy. It changes from time to time but mostly stays true." Painted in inks of color, a picture of a queen backed by soldiers in black and what looked to be a fierce shadow with wide wings sat upon a throne. A blue aura surrounded her in her gown of black and a crown of bone on her head. The words down the sides were in a language I couldn't read but I wanted a better look. Pinching the corner, I made to pull it towards me.

Wind filled the chamber, whipping cloth, flame and anything it could grab. Just as suddenly as it appeared, it died. A smoke the color of the aged paper bloomed from where it lay on the bed. Coalescing into a cloud that filled nearly half the room, we pressed back from it, waiting to see what it would do.

Flashes of blue streaked from it like lighting as a queen in all black came forward as if stepping from the fireplace. Behind her an army. And across the ceiling shadowed a giant beast. They clashed with men of red and white as if we and the furniture weren't in the way. Screams and roars filled the air as they fought right in front of us. Soon only two remained.

A queen in black and one in red. Vorpal sword in one hand, ball of light in the other, the black clad queen met her head on. Clangs of steel rang as their weapons met before the vapor was sucked back into the sheet laying on the bedding.

"What. The. Fuck. Was that?" Daniil spoke what we all were thinking. All were pressed to the walls, wide eyed and ready to act but to what effect, they had no clue.

Gently, Rabbit reached for the piece of the Oraculum. When nothing happened, he looked it over, flipping it over to see the backside too. A quick glance at me pressed to the headboard had him hastily rolling it and returning it to its sleeve. "No fucking clue."

Climbing back up on the bed, Rabbit patted where I had been sitting. When I refused to come from the fort of pillows around me, he nestled back in my lap, grabbing one of my hands and placing it on one of his ears. Not being able to stand the staring, I focused on the repetitive motion of stroking those long white velvet ears.

I'm not sure what he saw, but with a nod, he went on. "At the removal of the piece, the only thing the Oraculum has done is keep the future that was predicted right before this. A future that is coming to fruition. The royal lines are dying. No heirs, no pure Horunvendush heirs have been born since Alice was here last."

Leonid sat on the edge of his chair, elbows to knees, hands clasped in front of his mouth. Eyes on me and the rabbit. Shaking his head, "so a queen to rule all of Underland. But if the royals are dying, that leaves the current heirs and only one is female. Are you saying that inbred bunch of sickly psychos are to, what? Rule a united people? How the fuck are they going to do that? No one is going to go for that. Even the Dush hate their rulers."

"I think we need a little lesson on family trees real quick. Upon Alice's final return, she was pregnant. The child belonged to her late husband. The white queen and king had a daughter, Lily. The queen of Hearts had her daughter, Rose.

132

The red queen had no children but took on the raising of Rose, her niece, like her own.

"Now pay attention, because this is where it gets a little...messy. Anyways, the white queen has vanished. The poor white king is beside himself and needs a wife to raise his child, what better way than to marry Alice."

"Wait, wait, wait. Where did the white queen go? And why marry Alice? Kings don't need queens. Fuck, queens don't need kings." Toli was sitting on the back of his chair, feet in the seat but in the same pose as Leonid.

Toras was sprawled on the run now, his voice drifting up from the floor at the foot of the bed. "I know the answers to at least part of that. Kings, and queens, need heirs. And Lily was female and his only one. What better way than to marry the savior of Underland. The prestige and the ability for heirs since she was obviously fertile."

"And the white queen?" Daniil asked from where he was man-spread next to his brother.

Leonid was the one to answer him. "Dead. The queens were the power and bloodlines. He was nobody without her. What better way to have power than to get rid of the real power behind that throne."

Rabbit snapped his fingers and pointed in Leonid's direction without moving from my lap and the petting he was getting. "Exactly. What most have forgotten is that Alice is a queen too. During her trials on the visit before this one, she played a game of chess with the queens, working her way from pawn to queen. As she won the game, while finding a lost Lily I might add, she was crowned queen. Now we know there is already a White Queen and a Red Queen.

"What color doesn't have representation? Forgotten even now? Pushed to the back of memories in words spoken by the jabberwocky and Oraculum?"

Holding out my arm, I watch as the ripples reappear before fading. "Black."

Booping me on the nose, Rabbit pulls my hand back to petting him. "Right you are. Alice was the black queen. Or as she was declared, the obsidian queen. She never had a throne or kingdom. Her choice in arraignment to show who she was, the Vorpal sword. A blade black as night from pommel to tip. And if you look at the armies, white chessman of the Pale, Crimson Deck of diamond and heart. That leaves her?"

"A hell of an army. Adding in the bandersnatch and those that live outside Horunvendush rule. She would have been unstoppable." Leonid and Toras are nodding at what Toli just said as he is perched on the back of his chair, his tail on display and twitching.

"She would have. Had the white king not pushed her into the looking glass and then shattered it. He commanded all portals sealed and she never returned. Out of anger at being rebuffed, he struck all records from Horunvendush history of Alice's coronation and titles. He did take in her son, Lewis, raising him with Lily.

"I assume it was to tie them together in marriage but he was thwarted by a promise to the missing Queen of the Pale that her daughter could marry for love that stopped him from arranging it. If he had managed it, he would have all the power that was bestowed to Alice and whatever that power was that allowed her to walk between the worlds."

My turn to ask a question, "Lewis was a portal walker? A Wanderer?"

Nodding, Rabbit went on. "But Lewis was in love with Rose. And the red queen might have appeared benevolent, but she was just as shrewd as her sisters. To have that power would have been a boon. She encouraged Rose to build a relationship with Lewis. But Rose is the daughter of the queen of Hearts. And nurture over nature, she learned quite a bit at her mother's side. Rumors are that she spoke to her mother's head often.

"Rose didn't want a man at her side. She wanted it all, like her mother and aunt. So she took the pieces of the broken portal mirror, reassembled them and opened it once more. What she hoped to find, we don't know. Lewis caught her and as they argued, a group of young women tumbled through. Daughters of a Russian Emperor on the run from assassins.

"Fearing the king of the Pale and what he might do if he found out Wanderers had returned, Rose came up with the idea to take the girls to the Underlanders. Blame could fall on them should it be discovered and there was enough bad blood, it would be believable. At least to Lewis that was a good idea when it was jealousy that fueled Rose when she saw the way Lewis looked at one of the women."

"Even if she didn't want him, no one else could have him?" Josef yawned into his fist as we all nodded in agreement with another snap and finger point from Rabbit.

"So a wagon rolls into the village. Four women and a broken mirror accompanied by Lewis himself. Not knowing what to do with them, they are brought to Crone as no females are allowed in Temple. She takes one look at the oldest and declares her the mate of Lewis. Absolem performs the ceremony and bang, deal is done. Now most deals are for offspring. But we took a different payment that day."

"The mirror." Hanging above the mantle of the fireplace, broken but reset in the frame. As I look at the last portal out of Underland, movement appears when there is none on this side to be a reflection. Looking at my companions, none are looking where I am. Pushing it to the back of my mind as being tired after all I've been through, I look back down at the male on the bed with me.

With a smirk, Rabbit tips his chin up for scratches there. "Rose has a fit when Lewis and his bride return, as does the white king. That idiot is none the wiser where the bride came from. Her accent alone told she was not from our lands. Lily marries like many in her line to a cousin in an attempt to keep the blood pure. Rose has an affair with her Knave and has a daughter, the current Crimson Queen. Who then has her own children, with a lone survivor from infighting.

"Lily's sons, Arthur and Henry, both become king, both marry Lewis' daughter, the current dowager, and your mother." He looks up at me as I snarl my nose up at the thought. "There is something about mixing the line of Alice into either royal side. Absolem said it was a magic that prevented it. Preventing that power from being used by those not fit to wield it.

"Whether that is true or not, I don't know. What I do know is that there is a prophecy of our own. One many think is just a tale to keep Underlanders hoping that one day, we will be free. To have our land back. To fight when the time comes. Absolem was a male of many secrets. All that was ever recorded of it was the words in one of the oldest books out there."

Pointing to the other room, he takes a drink of my now cold tea I had forgotten beside me. Surprisingly the plate of treats and cup were still on the book and hadn't been spilled when whatever came out of that paper. "I'll paraphrase it since it is all in this flowery prose that just gives me a headache. Translated; the blood of a god will mix with that of Wanderer to produce the daughter to bring Underland back to the original people."

"It isn't Alina. She isn't the final female of a royal line." Toli's eyes hold mine as the others look to me on my throne of pillows, dressed in the finest of silk sheets.

My mind swirled as I thought back over all that had been said. That I was this prophecy come to life. Letting my eyes unfocus, I checked with whatever had woken inside me. It smiled. "One last thing, what am I?"

Rabbit hopped off the bed and swept into a deep bow. "You are the Obsidian Queen. Soon to be Queen of Underland. The power of a God and Wanderer flowing through your veins. And what we see manifesting in you, that is what returned to the earth, waiting for the rightful heir to use it to take her throne, to free her people. And I am honored to fight at your side."

Deck & Board

"I told you. You stupid, stupid girl. You just had to play with your food. Now look at you. Ruined. Not able to birth another child, not able to carry on any bloodline. All because you were petty and had to show you were stronger than a peasant. My son will not be having you now. None will. Men want heirs. That is their legacy, their way of being immortal. And we provide it for them, that is our power. I should have taken care of it myself."

Pain glossed eyes looked up from the chair next to the bed, following as the crimson queen changed the linens splattered in blood. Tossing a thick pad made from a folded blanket into the middle, Hortensia waited for Alina to crawl back in.

Pillows piled behind her, Alina pulled a sheet up her shivering form. The queen was right. She was ruined. It wasn't only men that needed children to carry on their lineage. A field doctor had turned up to aid her as a child came into the world with twisted limbs and features. Skin so translucent it showed the form of organs underneath. Heart visible as if under a thick gauze as it attempted to beat, lungs struggling to breath. Eyes without color had opened only to close as death took it.

As that thing had been pulled from her womb, Alaric's form had been carried into the castle on a shield, barely alive. She had attempted to go to him, be at his side like she had always been. Draw strength from each other. That bond built in the womb. When she was found in the hall outside his room, the medic had her carried back to her bed and worked to stop the bleeding. Passing out, she had woken to the news that the only way he could save her was to remove her inner female organs. Sobs tore from her chest as she considered Alaric and that his death would make her queen, but of what?

Bodies everywhere, buildings in ruins, people fleeing. A once mighty kingdom smoked and smoldered. Black staining the walls and walks of the Providence of the Pale. Where it once shone like a beacon, the Citadel was nothing but unstable columns with gaping wounds like missing teeth in the towers that had once housed generations of Whites.

Even the dead screamed at the destruction. As Alina laid her still born daughter to rest with her ancestors, the twisted remains of once proud people that led generations in Underland were scattered like someone had thrown a tantrum at their loss of a game, swiping the board clean. The babe was tucked into a niche with some long dead member's ashes of their bloodline, in the only crypt with some semblance of structure left.

Panting from the effort it took to move from bed to chair and back, Alina watched the bitch of a queen curl her nose up at the pile of soiled linens in the bathtub, drying her hands on her skirt as she came back in the room. "Oh, I know how you would have handled her. Off with her head. And then what? What of those plans you ranted about? How are you going to open portals now?"

Lips twisted in a snarl, Hortensia stood at the foot of the bed, looking down on what was left of the girl that would have been queen. "You want to play that game? Talk of plans? The girl that wanted to be queen of it all. I wonder how you were going to pass that child off as Tristan's?"

With a cruel twist of her lips, Alina motioned to the window and the crumbled place the child rested eternally. "That child? That child is all his. I gave him a babe and as the deal states, I am now his queen."

Tristan was in no state at her arrival to make much sense of, mourning the death of the babe he had thought his and the possible loss of his best friend. Barking a laugh, bending at the waist, gasping, the crimson queen looked at the woman struggling to get out of the bed. "That is not Tristan's child. That freak you buried this morning, that child is just a whiter shade of pale like you and all those inbred fuckers you call kin. Spreading your thighs for your brother. Oh, Tristan told me all about what he had seen. A smarter woman would have at least picked a donor that looked like the man she was going to trick. And it was for a live child. Death can't wear a crown."

"How dare you?" Affront thick in that statement, Alina used the post of the bed to support her weak legs as she faced off with the final queen of the Crimson line.

Void veil doing little to disguise the hate on the face underneath, the crimson queen looked down her nose, "how dare I? I'll tell you how I dare. I have seen every child that was put in the belly of every lover my son took. Death does not hide parentage. Skin golden like the sands on our shores, hair as black as night, eyes so deep brown that the shadows find no harbor. All bore his resemblance regardless of the mother. Want to try again?"

Alina trembled where she stood, hands grasping the cradle behind her. "You talk of parentage, I know what Tristan is."

"What is he? Hmmm? I'll tell you. He is the rightfully born heir to the Crimson Dynasty. Yes, he is Wanderer but at least his blood isn't fouled with the impurities that arise from fucking your own blood." Steps echoing on the marble floor, Hortensia paused at the door, "just as I know that that child's father lays dying in the next room. As I know that you and your brother fuck and when Tristan got done shouting across the throne room filled with my court, all in the kingdoms do as well."

Walls of sanity came crumbling with the scream that was sealed behind the doors.

***

"Tristan."

Hands buried in his hair, elbows on his knees, the man in the chair at the side of his once best friend looked up at his name. "Mother."

"What the fuck happened out there?" Arm pointing out the open doors that did little to relieve the smell of death, Hortensia waited for an explanation.

"Children playing at roles they aren't capable of handling brought on a power that we hoped to control."

Having not noticed the woman sitting at the side of the dying King, Hortensia startled. Angry that she was caught off guard, she turned on the dowager. "Ekaterina. How lovely of you to grace us with your presence?"

Dry snorting chuckles were her answer. "Your mother set this in motion with her need to know if she was to be one to fulfill the prophecy. If she had only taken Lewis to bed and made him her king, we wouldn't be here."

"No, we wouldn't be. Mixing of royalty and that piece of trash Overlander you call grandmother would have ended us all. My mother did what she needed to keep her power, her kingdom." Hands on her hips, Hortensia faced off with

Ekaterina over the body losing its battle for life on the bed between them.

"And your mother spreading her legs for the first man that she came across did that?" Pointing at Tristan still crumpled against the wall, she gave a sniff at what was supposed to be a king. "Poor breeding indeed. Can't even rid us of one female. No, he ran."

"I see that was a lesson you taught Alina just fine but she might have misunderstood a bit since it was her brother plowing her. Let me give you what I gave her. Truths in the form of pointing fingers. Want to talk of laying with the first thing that came along? My family wasn't the one fucking monsters. Making mongrels." Drawing up to her full height, Hortensia waited for Ekaterina's reply.

"Emrys." Cocking her head, Ekaterina waited at the word she had flung like a gauntlet at the other queen's feet.

Rolling her eyes, Hortensia crouched down in front of Tristan, brushing the hair from his forehead, "not my bloodline. I told you, we didn't bring that filth to our beds. No, his parentage is of Tristan's father's brother. That taint never entered my lines."

She was forgetting her plan to do just that with breeding the woman that had escaped to her precious son. Attempting to backtrack, to formulate a new plan. Grasping a handful of hair on the top of Tristan's head, the crimson queen stood, pulling him up with her. Shaking the man like he was a ragdoll, sneering into his face as his eyes widened at the mistreatment, she asked again, "what the fuck happened?"

Blubbering until he was shaken again, Tristan spilled it all as quickly as he could, fearing his mother and the rage that her veil didn't hide, rage that cost people their heads. "Alina didn't keep her. She took the maiden to the dungeons. Had her beaten and raped. She lost the child she carried."

Not exactly what she asked but it was information that hadn't made it to her as her spies were as dead as the majority of her army. She would remedy that shortly. With another shake, she prompted him to continue.

Tears running down his face, snot joining them before he wiped his armour across his face, Tristan spilled the rest. "We were set to meet, ready to take the Pale Citadel when something went wrong on Alaric's side. Devana appeared, killing the ground as she walked through us all. Animals were going nuts, it was taking all we had to control them. A boy spoke to her and she said something about beasts in the woods no longer hiding. Then she screamed."

Ekaterina now stood next to Hortensia listening to his ramblings.

"Alaric collapsed, men fell, animals too. And..."

With another shake, eyes rolling in fear, the whites too prominent as he stared unseeing out the balcony doors, he whispered one word. "Jabberwocky."

***

Ekaterina sat at the desk in the king's study, a large tumbler tapping on the marble as she watched Hortensia pace.

"It isn't possible. Alice killed it."

Raised in a manor on the edge of the pale kingdom, Ekaterina had been privileged to hear tales from the peasants and creatures that called themselves the people of Underland. Not to mention the stories her own father had told her of the visits of his mother. She knew that it wasn't like the other beasts that called their world home, not of flesh and blood.

With a smile, she sipped the bourbon, enjoying the bite of it. Her daughter was the chosen one. That beautiful baby she had brought into this world. Given into the safe keeping of

Crone and the priest that fathered her. Brought up in the teaching of the Underlanders. A woman of substance. Mated to a pride of warriors. Ready to take her place as queen of it all. Ruler of armies. Keeper of power that was beyond imagining. Wielder of the jabberwocky.

Smile turning conniving, she looked at the woman now standing at the windows. It wouldn't be her son ruling, marrying and breeding a queen of the people. No. It would be Ekaterina's daughter. With a harem in her bed and armies so vast none will stand in her way. "I told you. Power. And she that can harness it, won't be yours to control."

We're All Mad Here

Floating.

Body at the will of the pool of liquid that healed me, I just... float.

Needing time to absorb what I had been through. Needing time to absorb all the rabbit told us. Needing time to absorb I'm the answer to a prophecy. Needing time to absorb that I'm a goddess.

I just float.

Upon entering the water, my head had been pounding behind my eyes. My brain felt like it was beating to escape my skull. Sinking below the surface, I prayed for a little relief. Just long enough to catch my breath.

When my lungs screamed for air, I let the natural buoyancy bring me up. On a deep inhale, I relaxed into the urge and here I was. Brain clear. Just being.

Water rippled as a form entered the pool with me. Arms scooping me up into a chest, carrying my limp form from the water. Still feeling as if I was floating, I let his scent tell me who he was instead of opening my eyes. Peace was hard to come by and I wasn't keen to let it go just yet.

Warm fur, healing herbs, hearth smoke, crisp linens, magic. Purring, snuggling into him, I tipped my face up to Toli. Lips brushing mine, he returned my rumble of affection. Laying me on the moss, sinking with me as I held out my arms to pull him down. Deepening the kiss, licking into my mouth, Toli moved his weight off me to rest along one side, braced on his arm so he had access to all that was me.

Those long, elegant fingers spread over my hip, pulling me sharply to him, turning me so I was on my side as well. Running that hot palm over my ass, pausing to grasp it firmly, to my thigh, pulling it up over his hip.

Gloriously naked, he rolled his hips into mine. I breathed his name on a moan. Cock grinding into my mound, sticky cum smearing on my lower belly. Hot in comparison to that ladder of metal in his shaft. Trailing that hand back up, fingers ticking on each vertebrate before grasping me by the back of my neck.

Spine bowing, chin up, I gave him my throat.

Snarl ripping from him, teeth setting into the triangle of flesh where neck met the underside of my jaws, I felt him bite as he sunk his cock deep. Any lower and he would have crushed my ability to breathe. This bite would be one that was on prominent display. Purr still ticking away, my pussy clamped down on him.

Hips surging into mine, he rode out my orgasm, chasing it with another before those fangs released, tongue lapping the blood. Pushing Toli to his back, planting my knees into the deep moss, hands on his chest, eyes flashing, skin swirling with my inner powers, hips grinding into his, I used the male under me.

Rhythm stuttering, feeling each of those bars of metal, I ground my clit into his pubic bone. Close, so close. Hands gathered my hair, tilting my head back. Leonid stared down at me, fingers swiping the blood from where it pooled in the notch at the base of my neck.

Licking them clean, staining his teeth pink, he smiled down at me. "You need to mark him. Bite him. Give him back what he has given you. Blood for blood. Complete the link. Mate him. Bind him."

Yes. She hissed in agreement inside my head.

Riding the male, holding him down when he went to rise to meet me, I panted out as I chased my orgasm. It hit me, hard. Anatoli pushed off the claws sunk in his chest, moving to present for my bite. Grabbing his hair, I wretched his head back and returned the favor, less careful than he as I sunk my teeth in over his adam's apple.

Barbs sinking deep, we came as our beings twined together. Feeling all each other had to give. He crawled inside me, latching onto my soul. Releasing him, licking up the blood as it dripped down his chest, I shoved my tongue coated in his blood into his mouth.

"Good girl. Such a good girl. He feels good, doesn't he?"

Smiling, blood on my chin, I laid my head back against the thighs of the male behind me, "perfect. He feels perfect."

Chuckling, he petted my hair back from my face. "Just wait until we are all there."

I awoke as Toli's barbs released as I lay on his chest, still straddling his waist, his fingers carding through my hair. Kissing the muscles under my cheek, I sat up.

Josef and Daniil sat against a tree, heads back, napping. My gentle giants. Leonid leaned against the bark next to them, arms crossed, waiting. Pride king. Toras lay in front of them, hands behind his head, ankles crossed. Faithful servant.

"Who's next, my Queen?" Leonid's low voice brought the attention of the others to me.

I know I need to fix Josef. His self flagellation was radiating from him in waves so harsh they vibrated the air around him. But I needed Toras. Had been needing him since that night of my heat. Needing my teeth in him like his had been in me. Itching from him under my skin, crying out for the connection we hadn't forged.

Hands and knees, prowling over to the prone male, I licked up his shaft before swallowing down the length, gagging as he hit the back of my throat. Pulling off with a gasp, I waited until his eyes met mine before attempting it again. Lips bumping my fingers where I fisted the base to hold him where I needed him, I paused, letting my body get used to the invasion.

Licking back up his length, sucking the head, I could feel the bumps that would be barbs on my tongue. Swirling my tongue around his slit, I pushed against the opening. Fingers sinking into my hair on each side of my head, Toras hissed, back arching, thighs shaking as he fought the urge to drive deep.

Sitting up, Toras pulled me off his dick with a pop. Large hands cupping the sides of my face, he moved to kneeling before me. "Hmmm, kneeling for your queen."

Kissing me deeply, he maneuvered me to straddle him. "On my knees is where I would stay if it would make you happy."

Mouths fusing, I sat down sharply on his cock. Impaling myself in one swift movement, hissing at the invasion. Leaning back, I planted my feet on either side of his hips, hands on the ground behind me, a table for feasting his eyes. Veins in his neck popping, Toras threw back his head as he pounded into me. No slow warm up for us. Harsh and fast was our style. Fingers denting the flesh of my upper thighs, cock surging hard enough to bottom out, growl rumbling, Toras had me cumming in seconds without touching my clit.

Dominance was fucking sexy and these males had it in spades.

But I was a boss too. And she had needs. These males running around without my bite. Made her want to kill everything that moved, that wanted to take her mates away.

Grabbing Toras forearm, I pulled up to sitting, planting my knees back on the cool forest floor covering, I wrapped my arms around his neck. Lip lifting in a snarl at stopping him, he waited. Soft was not us and this position was too intimate for us.

Leaning in, lips brushing, he didn't see it coming. Marks should be prominent. Proudly on display. And this male had belonged to another first, even if he was to be a weapon. He belonged to me now.

Hips grinding, arms around his neck, hands in his hair to hold him still, I sunk my teeth into his bottom lip. Blood pooled in both our mouths as I pulled back a little, stretching the flesh in my teeth.

Big muscled arms wrapped around me, crushing me to his chest as he filled me. Cum running down into his lap, he set his barbs as my pussy milked him dry. Those twirls of smoke were back under my skin, Toras nuzzled my arm as they drifted by.

Leonid was back. Crouching down, he turned Toras' face to him, checking his pride member like he had done to Toli. "You're a little vicious thing, aren't you?" Trying to shake him off, the male submitted when a low growl rumbled from Leonid. Thumb gently pulling down on his chin to make sure I hadn't bit him too deep, the pride leader smiled before giving him a playful slap. "You looked unhinged before, now she has you looking positively mad when that scars up."

"Madness looks good on him." The correction of Leonid on Toras had the female inside me stretching towards him. But I had a plan and my twins were next. Pouting, she slunk back into her place inside my head. Nestling into the space under his chin, I chirped at the two resting against the tree. "You're next."

Daniil smiled wide, teeth on full display. I loved all the points, knowing they would sink deep. I could feel Anatoli and Toras as they settled inside me. Now I needed these two. And then the king of the pride, I'd make him my bitch, make him serve me. He just didn't know it yet.

Josef looked down at his hands in his lap.

That wouldn't do. No, he wasn't going to continue this moping. "Josef." Eyes jerking up to land on me at the tone of voice barked at him. Holding his gaze, I pulled before Toras' barbs were fully released. Hands slamming down on my hips pushed me back on the male I had just finished with. It was fine now, that little moment of impatience had had them letting go and I could now move without ripping my insides to shreds.

I would not crawl for this male. Josef thought me weak. Needing to be protected. Maybe I had been at one time. Not anymore. Power and strength that came from pain, from madness, had a way of building one up quickly. Standing in front of the pair, never having broken eye contact with Josef, I snapped my fingers and pointed at my feet.

On his knees, he bowed his head and touched his lips to my toes. Squatting down, knees spread, I put myself on display as I grabbed a handful of hair and lifted him up. Cum was seeping from me, running down my pussy before dripping to the ground beneath my feet. Josef attempted to move to lick it but I held him back.

"Another time. I want you to watch as I take your brother and when I call you, you will do exactly as I say. Do you understand?" Eyes rolled up from watching my pussy in front of his face to mine. A nod had the strands in my fingers pulling. "Good boy."

Daniil was on his knees, ready to worship me when I turned back to him. "Oh, two good boys." A shudder had them both dancing at the praise. This was interesting. I had been fucked many times since my heat and never had I thought that these two would like my dominance. None of my males really. We would be testing this out later for sure. Right now, I needed to complete our bonds and take the heads of our enemies, freeing our people.

Letting go of Josef, who placed his face back down, hands next to his head in supplication, I stood. Snapping my fingers, I pointed at the ground in front of me. Mimicking my movements when I took Toras, Daniil was at my feet quickly.

Toli had been deeper in the shadows so his markings weren't as visible but I could see these. Stripes danced on the skin of Josef as he shivered in want, a faded grey to the nearly brown black on his brother. Daniil's golden skin was warm under my fingertips as I danced them across his shoulders before pushing him backwards.

Mounting him, holding his bobbing cock up, teasing him in my folds, I leaned down to whisper before nipping his ear with a canine. "I want you both."

Eyes shifting to his brother who didn't move a muscle, Daniil arched an eyebrow at the request. "Um, sure. But you need to turn around, Josef is bigger and might..."

My shaking head had him trailing off. "I want you both. In my pussy."

That had the other three's attention. Leonid was shaking his head. "No. It isn't only the size. The barbs..."

Glaring up at him from where I sat on Daniil's thighs, Leonid stopped talking as the wisps twirled to life on my skin. Toli rubbed the back of his neck, pretending his leader hadn't just tried to tell me what to do. Before, yes, it would have worked. They weren't with the same woman I had been. Toras just copied Daniil's arched brow when I turned my glare on him.

Leonid got the full impact of her as I mounted Daniil. Sliding slowly down his thick length. A drop of cum beaded off the head of Leonid's cock as I made a show of taking Daniil. Rolling hips, I worked up and down him, taking a little bit more each time. Circling my waist as I bottomed out, I finally let my eyes close. Head back, hands on that pad of belly the twins sported over the abs of the others, I danced my hips on the cock inside me.

Panting, Daniil grabbed my hips, stilling me. "You want us both? You have to stop."

Josef hadn't moved. Reaching over, I petted his head where it rested between his hands on the moss. "Come on, mount your queen."

Sliding on his knees across the ground, he maneuvered behind me, straddling one of his brother's thighs. Bending forward, I set my hands on each side of Daniil's ribs, arching my back down like a stretching cat, presenting for the male that was bumping his cock against my already stretched pussy.

He slid up and pushed at the puckered entrance. Moving so he lost access to me, I sat and turned the best I could while his brother was inside me. Placing a hand on his chest, I shook my head at him. Being gentle with him seemed right at this moment as he wasn't quite sure what to do. We had all messed around in different positions and groupings but I had never taken any of them this way. "Lower. Both of you at the same time in my pussy."

Adam's apple bobbing with a swallow, Josef's eyes darted to mine before lowering back down. Nodding, he took a deep breath, that square jaw gave a twitch before he pushed me flat on Daniil. Hand sliding from between my shoulders, he held me at the lower back. Growling low, his cat making his stripes stand out a little more on his tattooed skin, teeth sharp in his mouth, upper lip splitting as his nose darkened and flattened.

Purring to encourage him, I arched as deep as I could go, lifting my hips, Daniil slipping nearly half way out. Pressure, a burning stretch and the head was in. Pants that interrupted the growls, Josef paused. Toras moved in my peripherals. I heard him spit just as the warmth of it hit right on my ass. Josef did the same, his fingers scooping it all, smearing around the length of him that had yet to make it inside.

Leonid fisted his hands and paced away, Toli following, talking low to him. Daniil's hands rested on my hips. Josef gave my back a stroke and pushed. A low yowl carried around the glen we were nestled in as my body gave to take these two. Steady in, Josef's hips met my ass.

Blowing out a breath, I turned my head on Daniil's chest to see Toras sitting on his ass next to us, knees bent, arms draped on top, hands clasped. That cocky arched brow they all seemed to be able to do met me. Rolling my eyes, I pushed up to hands and knees. "Move."

Having taken one in my ass and one in my pussy on other occasions, they knew how to move to make it enjoyable for all of us. Daniil out and Josef in, push and pull alternating. Moans turned to grunts as I lost the ability to breathe. Fingers slid between Daniil and I, rubbing my swollen clit that hadn't seen enough action this night. Not that she needed it with the way these males were making me cum without it.

Blinking at him, I watched Toras stretch to help. "You need to get off. They need to too. You're damn near split in two and have another male yet to take."

Turning my face, I nuzzled at the muscle on the right side of Daniil's chest. Shirts were an anomaly so these marks would scream ownership just as much as the ones on Toras and Toli. Sinking my teeth deep, Daniil nearly bucked me and his brother off as he came, barbs sinking.

"FUCK! You cocksucker. I can't... I'm stuck!" Josef wrapped his arms around my ribs and pulled me back as he sat down on his knees.

"Get you ass and balls off my leg, fucker." Daniil grabbed me, stretching me between them as he sunk his teeth into the top of my right breast where I had marked him. Laving it with his tongue as blood welled to the surface.

Leonid was back, pacing with his hands fisted in his hair. "What do we do? How do we get them apart?"

Toras tweaked my clit, making me twitch hard as the twins growled at him, before pulling his hand from where it was smashed between us. "Just like any other time. We wait."

Josef pulled me back to him, head nuzzling my neck. "I'm sorry, Devana."

Reaching back, I raked my nails over his scalp as his platinum curls sprung between my fingers. "Shhh, I'll fix it."

Four sets of eyes watched as I petted my male. I could feel Daniil and the worry he had for his twin swimming in my brain. A rustle of my creature had him pulling back at the intrusion he hadn't meant to make. I couldn't help the small smile at the startled look on his face. When his mouth popped open to ask, I gave a slight shake of my head. Later.

That had Daniil's barbs retracting quickly. Raising slowly, I let the two males slip free. Patting Daniil's chest, I moved off him. Taking Josef's hand, I pulled him with me. Pushing him into the tree he had been napping against, I jumped, making him catch me. I was sore. More than likely he was too, having had his brother's barbs in his cock.

But I needed to fix him. Calling to my power, I let it seep from my fingers as I wrapped my hands in his hair. Sighing, he let his head fall back on the bark. Projecting, I pushed love and forgiveness into him. I pushed the promise that the baby would come when we were ready. I pushed forever.

Pulling back, I waited for him to open his eyes. Glazed orbs of silvery blue met my dark ones. Lips pressing to mine, he lifted me with one arm under my ass, lining up with my weeping pussy. Dropping me, he slid in, walls contracting on him.

Like with earlier, he took over. The creature let him, knowing we needed this. Arms covered in veins, muscles tight as he lifted and lowered me on his dick, Josef licked up my neck to my ear. With a snarl, he nipped it. Knees hitting the ground, he laid me back.

Hugging his hips with my thighs, I let him lift me. Arching, I placed my hands on either side of my head and bowed up. Tongue morphing, the rasp of it on my stomach as he licked up my sternum had me purring. Being petted was my absolute favorite but being licked made my toes curl and no one licked me like Josef.

Teeth sinking into the opposite side of my breast, I hissed a breath out, cumming all over the male locked to me. Arm banded around my waist, he lifted, leaning back on his free arm, he tossed his own head back as I sank my teeth in over his heart. A heart that was mine for the taking. Link snapping into place, I gave an extra clench of my jaws before letting go.

Just to remind him that he was forgiven.

Purring, I was content on the big barrel chest of Josef, I padded my fingers over his stripes, tracing them when I was yanked from my warm bed.

Hissing and spitting, I fought Leonid. This was not his show to run. We were thigh deep on him when he swung me back towards shore before twisting and tossing me to the middle of the pool. I had enough time to gasp in a breath before I sunk under the surface. A glow spun around me as the pool did what it was supposed to do and I was pushing to the surface.

Rising, a wake behind me with the force of my movements, I made for the male that had retreated to calf deep water, arms over his chest in his favorite stance. With a scream, I launched at him.

Leonid caught me, plucking me from the air like I was nothing. Hand around my throat, he braced my back with the other, taking my weight so I didn't strangle. Slamming me to the black sands around the pool, he snarled in my face.

Teeth bared in a hiss, I bucked at him. Caught by surprise, he was shoved to the side, allowing me to escape. Spinning around, feet and hands planted in the moss, I crouched, ready to spring.

With a grunt, he flipped to mirror me. A cocky grin that made me want to kick his ass danced on his lips. "You had them. Now you get me. And I needed you whole." Smile fading, he snarled the next words at me, "taking two cocks at one time. Fucking stupid. You could have been shredded if Daniil had been able to cum."

Smirking, I shifted my hips, readying to push off. "Jealous?"

Air omphing from his lungs as I speared him back into the sand, I sunk my claws into his chest muscles. Rising my hips from where I sat atop his thick abdominals, I sank down on the cock that was standing at attention in spite of the fight.

Moaning, I pumped up and down his shaft, letting my now healed cunt grasp slick on him. Not as thick as the twins, longer than Toli, Leonid and Toras were alpha all the way to the lengths they fucked me with. Groaning, on the verge of cumming for who knew how many times this night, I was plucked from my ride.

"You want it rough?" Snearing into my face, Leonid tossed me to the moss. That was better anyway, sand was hell to get out of moist crevices.

Picking myself up, I dusted off the stuck particles of black that glittered in the low light in our cove. Holding out a hand, I beckoned with my middle two fingers he had watched me numerous times fuck myself with for him to come to me.

With a twitch, he shifted into full beast. Laughing, I sprinted onto the path that ran the center of the sanctuary. Tendrils escaping behind me, power surged from me, leaving a trail for him to follow. Picking up speed, I made to jump an altar when he took me down.

A mouth full of mane was my reward when I went for his throat. "Yuck, I'm gonna get hairballs. Be hacking like I licked your balls."

Snarling, beast fading to creature as he moved me to be bent over the altar. Hand between my shoulders, I heard him spit in his other followed by the sound of him slicking his cock with it. Pushing to no avail against the polished black glass like stone, I tried to wiggle away. "Wait, you can't, not like this. You have to be male."

Having followed us, the others stood around the table that was just the right height for what was to come. Toli squatted down at the side of the stone slab, scratching his thumb over his lower lip, "interesting fact, when an alpha, a pride leader, takes a queen, he does so in his half form. Makes the binding final for all those involved."

Toras stood next to Toli, arms braced on the top. At my quizzical look, he shrugged, "what? I might be an alpha but I'm no leader. More of a sigma, if anything."

A slap to my ass had me yowling like when I took the twins. That hurt and got my attention back to the male behind me. But when he pushed at a hole, it wasn't my pussy. Struggling, bucking, got me nowhere. More spit landed in the crack of my ass, running down to lube up the largest damn dick any of them sported as it popped in.

Hissing, mists swirling over my skin and now the table to twine around me and the male pressing into my ass, I laid down. I was not submitting. No, I would have mine.

Fuzzed skin meeting the hot cheeks of my ass from his spank, I braced for him to move. Leonid didn't disappoint. Out until just the head was inside, he slid back in with a little force, making me umph out a breath. Eyes on males that watched me be mounted by their leader, I stuck two fingers in my mouth, coating them in saliva. Pushing my arm between me and the table, I pressed and rubbed my clit.

Knowing I wasn't going to move, Leonid removed his hand from my back, using the table edge to leverage harder into me. Clit swollen, I pinched and rolled it. Lids drifting closed, I let the feelings build. Wave crashing over, I moaned deep as my body clutched the cock powering into me. Teeth snapping, he sunk them into the side opposite Toras' mark. Mouth so big from his half form, front teeth hooking my collarbone, back sinking deep, nearly to the middle of my shoulder blade.

Scream echoing around the trees, I panted as spots danced in front of my eyes.

Pulling from my ass, Leonid's cum painted my back.

I could do nothing but lay there as my blood dripped on the altar as he rubbed his offering into my skin.

"Devana?" Leonid was back in male form. Crouched where Anatoli had been, eyes worried. "Love? I thought you knew. Thought that was why you fought and ran. And when he took over, I couldn't pull him back."

Rising, looking at each of the males around me. I walked back to the pool. Diving in when I was deep enough. I let the glow wash over me.

Surfacing, Leonid was in front of me, washing himself off. Tossing his words back at him, I moved from the glade and back to the altar, with a nod at the stone slab, "my turn."

Leonid had stopped in the middle of the path. Toras and Josef each took an arm and pulled him to the altar. All four muscled him up on top like the sacrifice he was to be for me. Climbing up on the end where his head was, I straddled his face, sinking down. "Eat."

Cum from the four males holding him in place had filled me before his turn. Quite a bit had slipped out, been washed away with my dunking. But I was sure there was more.

Pausing just a moment, he latched on to my pussy and sucked. Bracing on his chest, I sank deeper, moaning as he drove his tongue in. Rocking, grinding my clit into his chin, I came so hard, fluid rushed from me, drowning him. Falling forward so I didn't smother him before I was done, I panted as my poor, tired pussy throbbed from yet another orgasm.

She pushed at me, the creature under my skin. Rising, I did her bidding. Reaching a hand out to Josef, he helped me stand over the prone male below me. Fingers clasped in his large ones, I gingerly stepped down the black stone, my reflection looking all kinds of wanton.

Turning, I sank to straddle Leonid's thighs. "When I tell you to, lift him and hold him."

Nods were the response as hands slapped down on the male that began struggling again.

Mounting the pride king, I took him in one motion. Arching, hands reaching for the sky hidden by the branches above us, I rotated my hips. This was about me. Hips rolling, clit grinding, I moved slowly, building up to my finale.

A hand glided up my torso, pressing gently between my breasts. Planting my hands behind me on Leonid's thighs, I opened my eyes to slits. Power wept from me, covering the males around me, the table. Toras knelt on the table at Leonid's head, hands holding him down by the shoulders, helped by wisps of my magic. With a toothy grin, I let my head fall back as the other males clambered up to help.

Josef and Daniil each took a nipple, sucking and biting the stiff peaks. Mounding up the flesh to stuff their mouths. Gripping tight enough to leave bruises but felt so good, helping me get where I needed. Healing waters or not, I was wearing out.

Toli tapped my lips with his finger, popping it in to swirl on my tongue before taking it to my clit. Rocking, using the slight forward curve of Leonid's cock, I fucked myself good. Hitting all the spots as I climbed to that peak, striving for one last moment of bliss.

He was close, I felt the barbs start to tug. Pants, growls, snarls came from the male spread under me. I answered him as I set forward, moving the males that had been helping. Hips grinding hard, I felt that crest just before the world imploded. "Now!"

Leonid was lifted to sitting as I came and his barbs hooked in. Arms held out to his sides, Toras grabbed his hair to hold him for my bite.

And bite I did. She came forward as I lunged. I wanted to mark him on the neck, in that thick muscle with ticking veins but she had other ideas. Jaws snapping, she left both sides torn as she pulled back. Mouth full of blood, I fell back myself.

I would have fallen from the stone had hands not been there to catch us.

Checkmate

Standing at the head of the table of arguing males, I watched the figure dismount, tying his mount off to a post at the tavern. Boots thudding the packed earth of the village that served Temple, raising small puffs from the dried out turf, he scanned the activity around him.

Ringing of the hammer on metal from the blacksmith rang in the air. From around a fire, the soft *schnik* of blades being sharpened by a group of males was almost drowned out by the chime of metalwork. Claws and teeth were all and good but you had to be up close and personal. Swords, spears, and other weapons of combat evened the odds. If the enemy used it, you might as well too.

Males in half and full forms walked around, greeting each other with welcome chuffs, preparing for what was to come alongside those still to take fur. Shields were stacked along walls and fences, four and five deep. Small groups surrounded small mock skirmishes to keep muscles warm and real fights from breaking out with so much testosterone floating around.

Striding into the yard of Temple, he stopped to cock his head at the work being done here. Among the bandersnatch were humans. Being organized and assigned positions for battle, working to pack supplies for the wounded with the priests. Women were mixed with the males and men at all stations. All were intent on contributing to the cause, fighting or support.

Drawing up short, he took in the doors. Damaged and off their hinges, they did little to hide the inner hall. A place that was once a mystery for those not of the faith was on display. In the center was a large table covered in a map with small carvings to denote where strategy dictated the battle would take place. We were done hiding and if these people were going to join us, they deserved to know what was being planned.

Cats of all shapes and colors shoulder to shoulder, male and half forms. Whites, golds, tans, blacks, clouded, rosettes, stripes, spots, solids; arguing over troop movements and predictions of what the royals might do. Straightening his shoulders, he pushed his way between the towering forms of my own two striped males in half form, one white, the other golden.

All eyes turned to take in the newcomer, many a snarl and bared teeth accompanied him bracing his fists on the table edge as he pretended to study the map.

"What in the ever loving fuck do you think you are doing here?" My voice had the hall going silent as I waited for the man directly across the table from me to speak up.

Eyes rising from the map, the knave of hearts, Captain of the Deck, cousin to the king of the Crimson, and the one who delivered my son and had him returned here so he could be put to rest, met mine. He had kept his word as one of the surviving priests had told me how they had cared for him, treating him with the utmost care like all those that were given to them for last rites. Cheeky grin spreading across his face, he had the nerve to wink at me. "Hello, love. Miss me? Thought I'd come and offer my assistance to the rightful Queen of Underland."

Josef and Daniil grabbed him before any of the others could thanks to the idiot shoving his way between them. Hand up before they could pop his head from his shoulders, I pushed my shoulders back and looked down my nose the best I could since all the males here were well over my head. "Inbreeding seems to be making you all stupid. What makes you think that we would want or need your help?"

"Because he has been working for us since he was old enough to grow hair on his balls." Rabbit spoke up from where he was sitting to the side of us on a table against the wall, having a tea party with himself I was sure was more whiskey than leaves.

Turning my glare from the white eared asshole who was ignoring us once more after dropping that bomb, I waited for the knave to speak. I didn't have to wait long, most were unnerved by what crawled under my skin and he was no different.

"Interesting. She is in there. You have them all fucking running scared trying to think up a secondary strategy."

Wisps drifted from my fingertips across the table to him from where I had my hands planted flat on the surface. Everyone watched to see what they would do. One demonstration along with the word of the Time Keeper, and everyone was following the chosen one in the bid to freedom. But they were all scared shitless of the power I could wield. Predators petrified of the bigger beast.

And then there was Toras. Not that I needed his help but the fact that one of my mates was the new head priest with magic fueled by Temple. Add in two of the biggest warriors to be bred in generations, plus a veritable king of a pride that bore the scars of my mate bite. And my cheshire. Myth made real with his corporeal form that was the thing of nightmares when he was loosed. We were all a force to be reckoned with.

"Sorry I'm not so trusting of just any man that walks up here, care to prove you are on our side? My fuzzy friend over there, far into his cups if the stack around him is any indication, might know you, but we don't." Having reached him, my wisps drifted up, pausing as if to look him in the eyes before crawling over him like a snake in a tree.

Rubbing his head on his shoulder when one moved over his ear, the knave smiled at me like my magic didn't scare him. "Let's see, where to start?" Having been released by Josef and Daniil, he tapped his finger against his lips as if in thought. "I can mention it was me that brought your mother's body back from the Crimson Palace. Me again that talked the red king from removing her head and displaying it like some trophy. Me that brought you your final mate."

Turning to Toras, he flashed that smile again, "sorry about that though. I didn't really want to just dump you there but I couldn't have anyone seeing me. And it worked out pretty good for you. Healed all up, mated to a queen, and looks like you got her father's blessing too."

Leonid grabbed Toras' arm as he made to move on the male offering half assed apologies.

Sighing in mock affront at Toras' response, he turned back to me. Ticking things off his fingers, now on the fourth one. "Me that brought your son back here so he wouldn't end up in a glass jar on some shelf for a royal to brag on. Me that warned Absolem that he had a traitor in his midst. With that, me that has been Absolem's true spy, giving him information so he can make the proper moves to bring freedom back to his people. Me that ran all the queen's leads on you into dead ends over the years. Oh, and me that has a portal that can bring you all into Crimson lands."

I was sure we were all comical in our shock as we watched him place a portal piece in the middle of the table.

"See, told you, on our side." Laughter came from Rabbit as he poured his whiskey tea into his saucer and slurped it up. "And he is your seventh mate." With a smack of his lips he went back to ignoring us, again, as we all turned our shocked faces to him.

Leonid rasped though his still healing throat at the drunken bunny the question we were all imminently wondering. "Seven? What do you mean seven? And if he is the seventh, where is the sixth?"

Squinting up at the males all looking down at him, Rabbit plopped a pink cupcake into a cup, stabbing it with a crisp strip of bacon. The table he sat on gave a wobble as he pointed around the room. "One, two, three, four, five, six, seven. Not hard to count that high, even for me at the moment. Did she addle your brain when she gave you that love bite?"

He had pointed at himself when counting the number six. Looking at the males around the table, mates and those that had knowledge of the battles that had been against the royals over the years, I made a decision. "Give us an hour. Eat, touch base with your prides, I'd say not to repeat anything you have heard here but I know that will be useless."

Room cleared, I marched over to the white furred idiot and yanked him off the table by his ear. A chorus of complaints and cries of pain followed me into the inner sanctum. We might have opened the hall and barracks, but these doors had stayed sealed.

Spinning on him, I watched him rub his ear, eyes big with tears I was sure were fake. "Start talking."

Sighing, Rabbit tossed his ear behind his head with the other. "Short or long?"

Knowing how long winded he was and that time was of the essence, I picked. "Short. And this had better be worth interrupting everything and spreading more gossip. Or I'll..."

With his hands on his hips, he leaned down, our noses nearly touching. "Or you'll what?"

Snapping my teeth at him, I shifted my eyes over to Leonid and back to Rabbit's blue ones.

Hands held up in front of his chest, he took a small hop backwards. "Fine. Court of seven is in the prophecy too. If you think of the white queen's court, you'll know the seats. King, rooks, knights, bishops. Seven major pieces in total."

Anatoli looked the Time Keeper up and down with a snort. "You? A mate? Where were you a week ago when we all fucked like, well, bunnies."

"I told you, I'm not into females. Now if you were offering, handsome, I'd join right in." Toli's eyebrows damn near disappeared into his hair they shot up so fast when the rabbit winked at him.

When he saw my raised eyebrow and the interest at the thought of watching him with another male, he gave the rabbit another once over. "Later."

Coughing from sucking in a breath of air too quickly, pounding on his chest, Rabbit looked around the circle that were all enjoying him being bested. "Well alright then. Just so we are clear, I don't do females. But I have no problem being in your pride, mate pack, whatever you call it."

Rolling my eyes, I asked a final question, "how do you know that you and him...," I threw a thumb at the knave.

"Emrys."

With a nod to the man, I went on, "are my mates?"

"When he found you in the dungeon, you should have ripped out his throat. A female in a vulnerable position, protecting a cub, is a lethal thing. Only mates can attend a birth due to that. Instead, you let him help." Unbuttoning and rolling up the sleeve of his silk paisley shirt that clashed horribly with the plaid waistcoat he wore, he held out his wrist to me.

Eyes bouncing from the offered appendage to his face, I shook my head with no idea what he wanted me to do.

"Bite it. I need to be bitten into whatever it is you call this." He circled his fingers at the others.

"So a full court. Five bandersnatch, one Time Keeper, and a man...Dush?"

"I'm neither. My father was a bandersnatch warrior that the red queen had captured in an attempt to breed her own in an attempt to take down Absolem. My mother was cousin of her Knave and one of her ladies in waiting. They were mates and what I was was hidden." This seems to be a night for revelations. Like the rabbit, he begins unbuttoning clothes, only it is his shirt that he is opening, pulling the collar to the side.

Shaking my head, I glance at the males around me. All are just waiting for my move. Acceptance and love radiates along the bond. Stepping up to Emrys, I pat him on the chest before taking his wrist and biting it. He takes mine and repeats the mark.

Raising the wrist of Rabbit, I stopped short of biting him too. "And how do you know that you are my mate? How do I know what you say is the truth?"

Sighing dramatically, he answers me with an eye roll. "Besides being older than you and being much wiser." That earns a snort from several of us. "Rabbits don't just let anyone touch our ears. Delicate things. Full of nerve endings, capable of hearing the change of wind before it ever arrives.

And the night you arrived, they heard what it whispered. Even if your father needed to be absolutely sure."

I offer my wrist to him, and together we bite down.

***

Reassembled around the table, Emrys points out where the portal will let us out. He has already moved the pieces marking smaller cuts of the Deck and the bulk of them and how they will move to reassemble. He has just finished laying out how we can bring them down like a house of cards when one of the males from a pride that was out on patrol when Absolem was attacked raises his hand.

"Are we sure we can trust him?"

Toras growls at the male, making him shrink back. Placing my hand on his chest, I turn to the table and all assembled that have chosen to follow us. All weren't here when we lost Father having been out on patrols, gathering cubs, or scouting enemy territory. When word spread what had happened, they had returned to find us, no Father, and several high ranking priests and warriors and innocent cubs being given rites. It had taken a lengthy explanation from the Time Keeper and me manifesting part of what now resided in me for them to get on board.

The thing about bandersnatch, they were led by a creature of instinct. And even if the male wasn't sure, the beast within was and it was calling out for justice. And freedom.

"She says we can. And so does my cat." Anatoli had taken up Rabbit's tea table and was reclined on it, flipping a dagger, catching it with his tail as it flicked on the surface beside him.

Most had had a run in with Toli's cat so that was all some needed. This male was a little more skeptical. From where she was tucked sleeping, my creature stirred. Smoke dancing over my skin, I waited for him to swallow down his fear. They needed something more. I understood that. Stepping back, I loosed the control a little to let him see.

Voice as if it was from the pits of Underland, deeper than even Rabbit's burrow, she spoke to him. "We can. If my bite doesn't convince you of that, maybe I can find something else that can persuade you that he is on our side. Do you have an idea of what that might be?"

Emrys cackled, clapping his hands in applause. "I knew she was in there. I knew I wasn't imagining it." With a deep courtly bow, he greeted her. "Excellency, how lovely to meet you. Your vessel is our queen and so shall you be."

Knees hit the floor as the males and men around the room bowed in the presence of what I was.

***

In the dead of the night, our forces moved through the portal and onto the same dirt I had decimated. All that remained of what would have been a spoiled child's temper tantrum were smoking masses where the dead had been burned.

Behind me and my pride was the whole that was Underland.

Numbers that rivaled those of the Crimson Dynasty and Providence of the Pale had quickly outgrown our little hamlet we had called home. The spades and clubs, the chessmen of black joining our ranks.

With a smile, I had handed the cloak back to the lad that had given it to me on this field when he had come to pledge. It was then I learned that the coin around his neck was the emblem of those that followed the Temple teachings in secret. A roaring lion's head on one side and the Jabberwocky on the other. Fitting.

As dawn broke, we watched from the trees that had embraced me, lending me their power as what was left of the armies of our enemies assembled between us and the lands they were sworn to protect.

"See, just as I said." Emrys knelt on one knee in front of me, to the left. Josef and Daniil side by side directly behind me, Leonid and Toras were to my left and right with Rabbit crouched down in front of me, an ear slipping in and out of my hands as I stroked it in thought.

What Hortensia had been hiding, a secret weapon that was more rumor than fact as they hadn't been seen in many lifetimes, stood with the ranks of men. Figures of flesh that should have been resting when their time here was done swayed and jerked unnaturally. Some were pieced together crudely when they had lost parts in past battles or it had just rotted off. With them, they might stand a chance as they made their numbers supercede ours. Curling my nose at the abominations, I gave a gentle tug on Rabbit's ear as I stepped out.

Dragging me down into his burrow as the rest had geared up, he had presented me with what I wore now. The outfit had had all my males drooling when I had returned topside. Leather with stitched stress points that would allow me to move freely covered me from the waist down. Leather plating over my chest and stomach gave me a form to rival the finest courtesan.

From my side hung the Vorpal sword. Its obsidian blade absorbing the light instead of reflecting it like those that stood on the already barren grasses. As I could feel the power of my creature in my veins, twisting with my organs, seeping from my soul, I could feel the Vorpal had a power of its own as it sang for blood.

Whispers had me cocking my head in an attempt to hear the words. Generations wielding it, taking lives, fueling it. She had been a little upset when I had strapped it on. It was after all what had taken her last life. A tiny cut and my blood smeared into the blade had her quieting as I showed her it was of no threat to us.

I had left behind two pieces.

The boots.

I wanted to feel the earth beneath my feet, the strength it gave to those who asked.

The crown.

When my people were free, I would wear it.

Dried grass waving in the breeze, smell of rot drifting on it, I waited.

From the ranks came three horses.

Riding center was Tristan. His armor still made me think he had forgotten to put on his skin and was prancing around more than naked. I hoped they hadn't killed the jubjub birds for his and many of the other crests I could see. To his left was Hortensia. Side saddle on the field of battle, glittering from the amount of gems that were weighing down her skirts and poor horse. On his right was a little bit of surprise but not enough to throw me. Alina sat in an outfit similar to the one she had worn the day I met her, shroud trailing down to nearly trip her mount.

"You're looking...well, Maiden." Tristan acknowledged me first as Emrys said he would. These rules and etiquettes were just as stupid as I told him I thought they were when he explained them, I waited for the others.

A sniff came from his mother. "A ragtag bunch you have assembled. Have you thought this through?"

Arching a brow, I looked over my shoulder. Barely visible from here, I looked at my people. My pride stood just outside the corpse in solidarity for me.

Alina tsked when she saw Emyrs. "In bed with traitors. Careful, you might find him doing to you what he did to us." Her eyes stopped on Toras next, "and madmen. Madness can't be contained. Like a tempest in a teapot, it will crack and spill out."

Finally, "Mother, Devana, Chosen One, Bloodline of Alice, Daughter of Absolem." My voice took on that deeper quality, "Queen of Underland." Horses dancing, I bared my teeth in a feral grin. "All are acceptable titles as I am no longer Maiden."

With a sniff, Hortensia hid the fear I could smell on her at the sound of the beast coiling inside me, taking another jab at my people. "Unity. An army with unity is stronger for it. I see no banners, no capes, nothing that says they belong together. Will fight together, for you."

Snorting at the best she could do in her fear, twisting around at the waist, I looked behind me once more. I could see the front lines now at the edges of the trees, waiting for the signal. Flipping my wrist in their direction, the shadows deepened. Toras' mad cackle danced towards us as the dressings of my people deepened until black. Sweeping me a bow with his top hat in my hands, he blew me a kiss when he straightened. "Better?"

"You killed Alaric." If I didn't know better, I would think that Alina had a little bandersnatch in her with that hiss.

Stifling a laugh, I mock pouted at her. "I bet you miss him. Who is filling your cunt now that he is gone?"

Yanking the reins of the poor horse forced to carry her spoiled ass, she led the trio away.

"Oh, Tristan."

Slowing his horse from a trot, he turned in the saddle to see what I wanted.

"It really isn't fair."

Turning his horse back to me, confusion written on his face, he called out. "What isn't?"

Twisting my feet into the dirt and grass beneath them, I asked if the earth wanted to help. Warmth trickled up my legs in answer. "That those who have died are made puppets. Necromancing is a nasty art."

Looking back over his side of the field and then at mine which had come a little farther from the trees, he smiled at the numbers. "Not really if it gives you the advantage. Maybe we will make you into one. You do have talents that I would hate to see die."

Nasty. His tone told me exactly what talents he would use of my corpse. Turning on him, I strode back for my pride and people. Before I was out of hearing range, I tossed one word back at him and his army. "Rest."

A cacophony of sound echoed behind me as I reached my pride. Leaning in, I kissed the scars Leonid wore with pride, nestling into his side as the rest watched with wide eyes what I had done to the souls forced to reanimate and serve against their will.

Emrys, sitting in the grass, arms wrapped around his stomach he was laughing so hard, filled me in. "Oh, they are pissed. You took out over half their forces."

Pulling back from Leonid and the kiss I had pulled him down into, I turned. "Interesting. Some still stand."

Easing his joints from the crouch he had been maintaining, Rabbit looked over what was left. "Sometimes, evil doesn't die. Men can be inherently so and it bleeds into their deaths. Those things down there care not that they shouldn't exist, only that they can continue spreading the disease of their actions. Spilling blood to feed the monster that still resides within."

Toli pulled his sword as he shifted into his other form. "Here, here."

Touching the closest tree and the shoulder of the closest male, I asked of the earth again. Protection, power. And peace should we prevail. With one mind, we walked forward. Pace quickening as they moved from the protective shade, running as the last cleared the timber, we met the armies waiting for us head on.

Screams. Blood. Mayhem. Death.

Fighting surrounded me. Having worked with nature for longer than the beast I held in the frail shell that was my body, I used it as she howled to be let loose.

"Devana!"

Alina's scream of rage had me turning from defending myself against a patchwork monster that was once a man, now mixed with the parts of bandersnatch. Vorpal sword slicing air and his head clean off had it crumpling as I met my stepsister head on as she tried to run me down with her horse.

Rearing, it threw Alina as it turned in fear from the beast in front of it. As she was swallowed by the tide of bodies, I searched for Tristan and Hortensia. Finding neither, I tugged at the bonds. Exhaustion pulling at them, they were fighting around me, to get to me as we had been separated.

Toli broke past several bandersnatch that were attempting to shield me, pulling me into his arms. Nose pressed to his throat, I breathed him in for just a second to reassure he was alright before pushing off to swing at a man wearing the red armor of Deck.

Sword slicing him in two, I pressed my back to Anatoli's. "You need to do it. For them."

Shaking my head, I took out another soldier, this one in white for the Pale. Who dresses their army in white? At least you can't see the blood on those of the Crimson.

A flash of long white hair caught my attention too late. Gasping, Toli sank to his knees, handle of the knife in his ribs in his hand as he stared up at Alina.

Chaos and destruction rained down on them all as I lunged, only to have her spin out of my fingers and dart through a portal, slamming it shut behind her.

I snapped.

Clouds filled the sky as lightning so blue it hurt the eyes to look upon streaked down. Craters left where it had hit, the earth scorched. Flinging my arms out, back bowing me nearly in half, I let her loose with a scream that shook the foundations of the Pale castle to the right of where we were fighting, crumbling it to rubble.

Over the near constant thunder came a sound that had many clapping their hands over their ears. Sky lit with a bolt of electricity so blue it was nearly white, the outline of the Jabberwocky was visible. Wings, scales, and teeth screeched from the clouds with a clash of sound that shuddered the earth where we fought. Maw open, she devoured Deck and Chessman, noble and wraith.

Swooping high, battlefield devoid of those against us, she coalesced into the mist that danced along my skin, pouring back into me with enough force to send me to my knees.

Fighting for air and against the darkness creeping into my vision, I pulled Toli's head into my lap, petting the hair back from his forehead. "Please."

Warmth filled me where the rain chilled as the earth granted me the answer to my prayer. Placing my hand on his chest, I pulled the blade with the other, plunging it and his blood into the earth as an offering of thanks.

"Devana, Goddess." His hand on my cheek, I blinked my eyes open to see Anatoli whole. Rising to knees, pressing our foreheads together, we shared breath as we recovered.

Rabbit moved into my field of vision. His fur was blackened in places, covered in blood in others, a sword in his hand. "You know your name is an interpretation of the word devine and is for the goddess of the hunt and nature."

Huffing, I let him pull me up. Nodding to his appearance, "thought you were only here to observe and report."

"Couldn't let you have all the fun." He shrugged, turning to take in the scene around us.

Sizzling announced the opening of a portal. Emrys stepped out with a struggling Alina by the hair. "Brought you something."

Shroud ripped, tail of it covered in gore, one of the horns of gold broken and hanging down her back, Alina glared up at me in her armour now stained grey and pink from battle. "I'll kill you. You took everything from me. I was to be queen of it all!"

Toras picked up the Vorpal sword where it lay at my side, "you abused my mate and killed my son. Normally, I'd hand her the torch and let her burn the world down herself, but I think I need a little light in my life."

Whistle of obsidian and the thump of a head hitting dirt was all that was left of Alina, would be queen.

Leonid pulled me to my feet, tucking me back into my favorite place against his side. Emrys' portal was open.

Healers were coming through as those well enough to make the journey themselves went back. We had lost brothers, friends, too many as any death was too much. But we had won.

"Where are Tristan and Hortensia?"

Eyes scanning the fallen, Rabbit pointed into the distance. "There."

Horses whipped to full speed, Tristan and his mother were fleeing back to their palace.

Oh, hell no!

Reaching out to them, arm shaking, mists pouring from my fingertips, I pulled.

Landing just outside the metal portcullis, we marched after our prey. A sound from Rabbit had me glancing at him. On a pike was the head of Haigha. One of his long grey ears was missing, his face frozen in anguish. Toras wrapped Rabbit in a one arm hug, pulling him from the sight of one of his remaining brethren.

Tristan and Hortensia were fleeing up the stairs in the bailey of the castle as I stepped from the void, smoke pooling around my bare feet. Turning, Tristan abandoned the doors he was trying to shut on us, his fear pulling a smile from me.

Pride at my back, marching up the steps, I entered the ugliest castle I had ever seen. Red and gilt everywhere. Ignoring the atrocious decor, I followed the sounds of my prey. A door at the back of the throne room was their aim.

Flicking my hand, I swept them off their feet, bodies slamming into a dais where two gold thrones sat. Doors and windows slamming. No one was leaving without my permission. Pulling Tristan to his feet with a crook of my finger, he drifted towards me, toes dragging. "Coward."

Hortensia was pulling herself to her feet with the aid of the biggest throne but I kept my focus on the man in front of me. "I have so many reasons to kill you. You, however, are not who I want."

Flinging him to the side with a twitch of my fingers, he lay on the marble, unmoving.

Feet leaving the filth of battle on the mirrored floor, I strode up to the crimson queen. "It was all you. And for what? What do you have to show for it?"

Perched now on the throne, Hortensia straightened her spine, attempting to stare me down. Her gown in tatters around the bottom. One of the sleeves missing completely. Her crown lost on the field. With a sigh, she pulled the fitted veil off.

Eyes nearly the same shade as the walls met my earth dark ones. Head bald of hair, covered in scars that wrapped around her neck, creeping onto her face. Pointed teeth bared at me, she tossed the fabric to the side after a look at Tristan. "He was always a disappointment. Much like his father. But what was a mother to do? I had to love him. What was a queen to do? He was the heir."

"My mother..." I began.

"Deserved it. I needed her to remove the curse. Allow him a child so there might have been hope. While I was living to guide it to rule as I knew he was too weak to do it properly. I knew what she was, knew the power she had. She lied, she just didn't want to. I needed to make an example of her. You had to learn that when it was time for you to be called, you would do all you could to be spared her fate."

Slowly the room darkened. From me poured great billows that filled the space. Hortensia attempted to climb the throne to keep it from touching her. Coughing, she clawed at her chest and neck. Blood dripped from her nose.

Falling from the chair, her thrashing falling silent, I walked from the hell that had taken my mother's life.

***

Rolling my shoulders, I grabbed for the crown that slipped from the movement. I had yet to become accustomed to its weight and feared I never would.

"Do I have to wear it? Today isn't about me."

Rabbit stepped up next to me and adjusted the bones so they sat more securely. "Every day is about you. And before you say it again, no, you cannot give it to Leonid. This was your father's and his people's before him, whoever they were."

Emrys lay sprawled in Rabbit's bed, watching us as Rabbit made sure I was ready for yet another ceremony. It would seem that he wasn't into females either.. "He never wore it."

Toli sat in his favorite chair, paging through a book so big it rested on either arm. "Not to question how you would know, but no, he didn't."

"Absolem didn't for a reason and you can't use it as you are in fact, Queen." Exasperation laced Rabbit's tone at having to have this conversation again.

Emrys stretched and then burrowed back into the bedding. I was certain he was nude in there. "Father was a priest and priests didn't need arraignments."

"Father was a god and even though some might want to shout who they were with ostentatious displays, he preferred to be more subtle." Toli spoke the next part without taking his eyes off what he was reading.

My eye roll was ignored as Emrys sat up, revealing he was in fact naked as he got out of the bed to dress. "And he was never a king. Father was just..."

"Father." I finished for him.

Huffing at having us steal his chance at a lecture, Rabbit lifted the hood in my tunic and set it so that it draped on the back of my head, not covering the crown in any way. The spine of some long forgotten creature made up the band, setting low at just my hairline since it was meant to fit the head of a god and not his half breed daughter, that may be a goddess reincarnated. From it rose what was obviously fingers to make the points. Not a gem or piece of precious metal decorated it. All bleached bone and natural age to make it stand out against my dark hair.

Not that I wore it all that often. It wasn't like I needed it for people to know who I was, my shadows did that. And if those didn't, the entourage did.

Twin bandersnatch being a rarity, Josef and Daniil were recognized far and wide and always at my back. Anatoli's moods had leveled since his near death but then spiked again with the birth of our first cub eminent, his spectral tail and ears always on display now.

Emrys was the normal one, blending into the background and that was what made him the perfect spy. Rabbit stayed in his warren of tunnels but when he did appear, his eccentricities caused quite a stir, often in the fashion sense.

It wasn't even Toras these days being the center of attention. Father had rarely left Temple but you weren't going to tell Toras that. No matter how close to nature I could make it, he wasn't being shut in. I knew it was from his time in the queen's dungeons. There was a plus side to it, the people loved it and him, bringing them back into the original fold of what Underlanders had been before. Sure, they gave him a wide berth as he was still all growly and would sometimes shout an 'off with her head' or 'down with the bloody Red Queen'. It sure kept me humble, reminding me I didn't want those phrases aimed at me.

No, it was Leonid that had all eyes on us. Fully healed, he wore his mark of the Jabberwocky with pride. Mate marks being what they were, this one for sure screamed he belonged to someone where others were more subtle. His voice wasn't quite the same, there was a rasp that sent shivers through me to settle in my pussy when he turned his attention to me. That was all and good and not public knowledge. No, it was the role in my court we would be making official today.

Not that I needed a king or the people were demanding one, each of my mates had had a ceremony in the last months as we sorted where they sat on my court. Josef and Daniil being my Knights of course and Toras and Toli my Rooks. Rabbit declared the roles of Bishop his, citing that being the Time Keeper and a mate making him worthy of two seats. We humored him as it kept people from gossiping over who the other member of my court would be as we had no intent of adding another.

That left the king. In this game, he was supposed to be more important than me. It had taken us all this time to convince Leonid to take on the role due to not wanting to remove any of my power in the eyes of the people. He would have been happy with a bishop or rook position but the others snatched those up, attempting to force him into the role we all knew he was born for.

Bare feet leaving footprints across the hall from the soft damp that was the moss of the sanctuary, I walked out to address the people gathered around the front of Temple. The village had grown in the last year as we made the seat of our power here, dismantling the castles or what remained of them for the use of the people.

Glad I had opted for the leather leg coverings in the chill spring air, I smoothed the front of a split thigh tunic over my distended abdomen. The cub kicked, rolling to find room that wasn't there. He had rode into his first battle with none of us aware of his presence.

Cheers rang through the trees at my appearance. Pride around me, lacing my fingers with Leonid's as he stood in his place on my left, I gave them a squeeze as he looked down at me. Smiling, we gave our people what they needed.

Unity in freedom.

The Wrong Alice

beep

beep

beep

"See, there has been brain activity."

Doctor Carroll snatched the tape from the hands of the nurse, walking past a cracked mirror over the mantel, stepping to the windows to make sure that what he was seeing wasn't a trick of the low lighting.

"Doctor?"

"Doctor?"

"Doctor?!"

Jerking up from running the strip of paper through his hands, Lewis blinked owlishly behind the frames of his glasses at the woman wringing her hands at the bedside of her charge.

"Does this mean she is waking up?"

Stepping to the opposite side of the bed that had sat in the parlor room of the country estate of the Liddell family for as long as he could remember, Lewis prised open one of his patient's eyes, flashing a penlight to check for any kind of response. "That would be preposterous, I inherited this case from my great grandfather..."

Head cocked to the side, eyes squinted, mouth parted as if to say something, the nurse paused at what she had just heard. It took her a moment to process that statement. And then things began clicking.

The huge non-disclosure that her lawyer couldn't make heads or tails of except for the part where she was to live here, no contact with the outside world other than those that came to care for the house and the doctor in charge of the patient. A whisper would result in undisclosed repercussions.

Her background was picked apart in such depth that they knew she had fallen from an apple tree at the age of nine and broke her arm the day her parents died in a car accident. Being raised by a reclusive elder relative as her only surviving member of her bloodline had given her the ability to become a private nurse. Was childless due to a hysterectomy as a teen from severe endo. Being dumped at the altar, thrice, kept her without a spouse, as the hamlet she was from saw her as a bit of a jinx when the third time proved it was not the charm.

Not a soul spoke to her. If she needed something, it was brought in after she left a note or list of it in the kitchen. Meals were taken here, with the woman in the bed her only companion, brought on a tray and left on a side table just outside the room. Guards watched her with lethal looking firearms should she step outside for her daily allowed exercise.

"How? How is that possible?"

Head jerking up from his ward, Doctor Carroll took in the woman across from him. "What?"

"You said you inherited her case. From your great grandfather. How is that possible? She looks no older than her late twenties. That would make her..." Doing quick math in her head, she blanched at the number, causing it to come out a croak, "one hundred and eighty-five."

"Pish," the word hissed out at her, making her take a step back, "you misheard me."

Head shaking, bun flopping as it came loose, she denied him. "No, no I did not. How is this possible?"

Arms crossing over his chest as he sighed at the wide eyed woman in front of him, Lewis gave in. Who was she going to tell? None here cared who lay in this bed, only that they got their stipend. "I know not how it is possible, only that it is. I was told only that I was to care for her in her comatose state. The notes I was given told of some drink or food that she consumed on her travels and held them responsible, though she never gave details as to what they were other than tea, cake, and some rancid tonic. Travels that she returned from only to fall into this..."

Waving his hand, he encompassed the angelic woman between them. Pale hair nearly to her waist in a thick braid over her shoulder. Nearly translucent skin in spite of the sunlight that the afternoon bathed the room in. Frail form swamped in the twin bed as she lay there, her only nourishment the bags that were drip lined directly into a port in her abdomen.

What got all who saw her was her youthful looks. Not a wrinkle marred her face. Not a blemish took from the beauty of the porcelain complexion. The only color to her was the pale pink of her lips. Rich deep brown eyes would greet anyone who was given her care as eye drops were part of the routine.

"I can't...she just can't..." Raking her hands into her hair, ignoring the pins as they hit the floor and the mess came tumbling down. Fingers running down her face, digging in, distorting the flesh, down her throat leaving welts, she clawed at her chest. Gaze looking for what was hurting her, she took in the strange uniform request, seeing it truly for what it was. Long sleeves with a skirt that reached mid-calf, dark stockings and low heeled boots. Hat resembling something of a boat and an apron covering from the neck down. All to be pressed and starched. A nod to a different era. An era long gone.

"Pull yourself together." Voice cracking at the sharpness he delivered like the slap it was supposed to mimic, Doctor Carroll gathered up the readout of the brain activity and his coat. "I will return tomorrow to begin tests."

Looking around the room in disbelief, gaze falling to the woman looking more like a princess waiting to be kissed awake than anything, the chair barely caught her collapsing figure as her knees gave out.

Placing his hat on his head, Lewis nodded to the guard that held the door to the right side of his car open. Sitting behind the wheel, he went to pull it to, when he paused. Gaze ahead at the orchard just visible in the distance, he spoke four words. "Mad as a hatter."

Sunset that evening was disturbed by sounds that was heard by all however disturbed not a being on the property except the cat that had followed on ghost like paws to witness where the guard led the nurse.

CRACK

thud

shnik-thump

Madness

.

Review

STARTED

FINISHED

OVERALL ☆☆☆☆☆

SPICE 🌶🌶🌶🌶🌶

WRITING ✒✒✒✒✒

CHARACTERS 👤👤👤👤👤

ENDING ♡♡♡♡♡
*EVEN IF A CLIFFHANGER

NOTES, PAGES, REVIEW

_____
_____
_____
_____
_____
_____
_____
_____
_____

About The Author

The wilds of Appalachia are not big enough to contain the mind that is S.L. Simmons. Instead, she dreams up places where her characters can live out their own happily ever afters because she is living hers.

If you want to know the story of how she and her husband came to be together, feel free to ask. It reads like a missed chance/lost love/reunited trope that will have you saying, 'that would make a good book'. Yes, she is married to a real life *guy from the book*.

It all started with a song that would not leave her alone resulting in a story writing itself in her head before ever seeing the light of day. The voices have multiplied and so have the books. Don't be quick to pigeonhole her into a genre or trope though. She has several works in progress that differ from her breakout series of Mistletoe Fails. Contemporary holiday to paranormal to alien peen, she has a whole brain of stories to tell.

With an OCD and ADD brain fueled by caramel mochaccinos, the space around her protected by a pack of doggos, she writes out the stories that pop into her head at random times.

Where To Find Her

The best way to keep up with S.L. Simmons is on her website
www.slsimmonswordsmith.com

Blog, calendar of events, merchandise; all there and more.

www.ingramcontent.com/pod-product-compliance
Lightning Source LLC
Chambersburg PA
CBHW071508170626
46811CB00007B/2773